Hard Rock Fling

A Rock Star Romance

(Darkest Days Book Two)

by Athena Wright

ISBN-13: 978-1542762397

A note from the author:

This book contains mentions of self-harm. Readers should proceed with caution

Chapter 1

The spotlights flashed a kaleidoscope of colors, bright and hot. The crowd chanted, a dull roar of voices. The band remained backstage, ready to greet their adoring fans. Everyone waited in anticipation.

And I was the one they were all waiting on.

I scrambled around in boxes and totes, tossing accessories to the floor, not caring if they got dirty. Panic set in. What if I couldn't find them?

There. Underneath a pile of belts. Two pairs of identical sunglasses. I snatched them up and ran.

Five band members stood surrounded by assistants and interns, waiting for their cue to go on stage. Their lead singer looked out at the audience, scowling and irritated at the delay. The bassist and drummer spoke quietly to each other in hushed tones, mentally preparing themselves. As for the two guitarists, they paid no attention to the audience, or their fellow band members, or the barely-controlled chaos backstage.

Ian and Damon Drake, twin guitarists of hit rock band Darkest Days, were too busy flirting with the interns.

"*Damian*! I brought the two of you distilled water, not sparkling." A young assistant, a girl around my age, handed each of The Twins a bottle. "I know that's what you both like."

Since no one could tell them apart, everyone just called both of them *Damian*, a portmanteau usually reserved for celebrity couples.

"Aw, you remembered?" one of the twins purred, cupping her cheek. I could hear the girl's heart explode in her chest. "Such a sweetheart." He ran a finger down her throat, playing with the exposed collarbone peeking out from her tank top. "You know what else I like? Precious girls like you. Thoughtful. Sweet." He leaned toward her, noses practically bumping together.

"Your guitars." A crew member about a decade older brusquely hip-checked bottled water girl. She stumbled a few feet to the side. The poor girl blinked rapidly, dazed from her encounter with one of The Twins.

The guy handed a black guitar with a red fretboard to the twin on the left. He handed the second guitar, identical aside from the blue fretboard, to the twin on the right.

"Awesome, thanks," both twins said at the same time, sharing a sly smile. As soon as the crew member turned his back, they switched guitars.

"Anyone seen Damian?" I heard someone shout from across the room.

"They're back there," the crew member called, jerking his thumb toward the twins.

"Send rhythm guitar over here for a second. We gotta check this amp distortion."

The crew member looked back and forth between the twins, befuddled. "Uhh... which one's that, again?"

"Don't know, don't care. Just pick one," the voice called back.

"Excuse me." I tried to push between the crowd of assistants. "I need to give The Twins their sunglasses." They couldn't go on without their trademark shades.

One of them was busy fiddling with the leather wrist cuff covering his forearm and didn't hear, but the other, the one who flirted with bottled water girl, gave me a wink.

"Thanks, sweetness." He plucked a pair from my hand with an easy grin and stuck them on the top of his head.

"Damian, get over here." The drummer lifted his chin with a nod, calling The Twins over. "There's a last minute change with the setlist we need to talk about."

Before they could saunter off, I called out.

"Wait, Ian!"

The Twins froze mid-stride. Both turned around slowly. The twin on the left narrowed his eyes at me, looking puzzled, almost bemused.

"What did you call me?" he asked, giving me a slow once-over.

My heart skipped a beat at the piercing look in that brilliant green, bright and glinting.

"Sorry," I blurted out, suddenly nervous. "I couldn't find the right sunglasses so I wasn't able to give them to you earlier and you can't go on stage without them or else my boss will be upset with me." I snapped my jaw shut, ceasing my rambling.

"You want to give Ian his sunglasses?" Ian asked.

"You sure you already gave Damon his?" It was Damon who spoke this time.

I frowned, confused, and glanced back and forth between the two of them. "Yeah. Damon's wearing his sunglasses," I said, nodding to one twin, "but I still need to give Ian his pair." I nodded to the other.

The Twins stalked towards me as one. I nearly backed up, so intense was their stride. When they were less than two feet away, they stopped. I was faced with two probing stares.

"Who are you?" they asked in unison. My heart jumped in my chest.

"No one. I mean, I'm just an intern. I'm not important. Just ignore me. Sorry."

The contemplative look they gave me, heads tilted slightly to the side, was enough to make me shiver. I'd never had the full attention of a famous rock star before, let alone two. Stage presence was one thing. Two pairs of eyes examining me like a puzzle to be solved was something else. It made my stomach flip.

Although Damon's green eyes usually glinted with mischief, they were narrowed, displeased. This close up, flecks of deep blue around the iris made his eyes darker than normal. Ian's eyes, on the other hand, green with flecks of gold, were softer, brighter. I could feel him sizing me up.

I wondered how many girls got close enough to notice the difference in their eyes. Probably more than I cared to guess. They must have been fraternal twins, to have different colored eyes. They were so similar, though. Like exact copies of each other.

The Twins shared a glance. Damon's brows furrowed. Ian's lips twitched with amusement. After staring at each other silently for a few moments Damon shrugged and walked off. Ian stayed behind.

That considering stare turned warm. He took the sunglasses from my hands and flipped them around until the frames faced towards me. Two gentle hands hooked them around my ears, adjusting until they sat perched on my nose. A finger trailed down the bridge of my nose to my lips. My stomach leaped into my throat.

"You keep up the good work, sweetheart."

His voice was low, teasing, with a hint of something more. Something heated. He leaned in until we were cheek to cheek. I tensed up, holding my breath. My hair ruffled as he spoke quietly.

"Your boss hired a very perceptive intern."

He straightened his back, lips leaving a tingling sensation where they'd touched my ear.

I made a motion to take off the sunglasses. He grabbed my hand and interlaced our fingers. That small touch sent a spark shooting through me.

"Keep them."

"But what are you going to wear on stage?" He still held my hand. "My boss will be angry with me if you go on without them."

He smirked and pulled an identical pair from his back pocket. "I've always got a spare. Don't worry. I'd hate to see your boss fire you." He stroked the back of my hand, an intimate caress. My legs went shaky for a brief moment.

Ian smirked. Despite the fluttering in my stomach, a contrary feeling came over me. He knew exactly the effect he was having on me, that playboy jerk.

I forced myself to stand up straight, locking my knees. "I'm surprised you care about some random intern."

He met my gaze for a brief moment. In those few seconds, his eyes glimmered with something I almost couldn't identify. Curiosity?

"I wouldn't want a pretty girl like you getting away."

"I'm sure if I got fired you'd find another pretty girl within seconds."

He grinned and flipped the sunglasses between his fingers. "Seconds? Damn, I know I've got good game, but seconds? I'm flattered."

"It wasn't meant to be flattering."

His mouth popped open, astonished, before laughing. "Should I be offended, then?"

"Just making an observation."

"Hm." Ian eyed me up and down. "I did say you were perceptive."

"I don't need any special insight to know you're a manwh—" I bit my tongue before the words could come out.

"What was that?" Ian teased. "Were you just about to slut-shame me?"

"No!"

"I think you were." He shook his head and made a tsk sound. "You shouldn't listen to tabloid gossip, you know."

He cupped my cheek, just like his brother had with bottled water girl. Maybe it was their signature move. His thumb brushed my lower lip. A jolt of electricity ran up my spine. My body warmed to the core. I tried to think through the haze taking over my brain.

"Then again," he said, "they do say there's a grain of truth to every rumor."

"Hey Damian!" The bassist called out. "Quit flirting. We're going on soon."

He pulled back. My lungs began working again.

"Your adoring fans await," I said, trying not to sound breathless despite my rapidly beating heart. "You better get going, Ian."

He tilted his head, giving me one more look, bemused, but with a heavy weight behind it. "Take good care of those shades, sweetheart. They're my favorite pair."

I watched through tinted lenses as he strolled off and joined his band members. The Twins shared a quick look and turned their eyes to the stage.

When my stomach stopped tumbling over, I took the sunglasses off and clutched them in my shaking hand. I could still feel the touch of his lips on my skin. The brush of his thumb against my mouth.

The audience burst into cheers. The concert had started.

I let out a slow breath. No need to freak out. I'd found the sunglasses. I'd delivered them to The Twins in time. No reason to panic.

No reason aside from the look in Ian's eyes whenever I said his name.

Chapter 2

After my encounter with Ian, I forced myself to take deep breaths, trying to calm my heartbeat. It was no use. My pulse points were throbbing — not to mention the throbbing in the other, more intimate, parts of me.

I glanced around to see if anyone noticed my reaction to Ian. Thankfully, the staff and crew members were absorbed in their own work. Besides, they were no doubt all used to The Twins' flirting. It meant nothing.

When my breathing was even, I tried to put the whole thing out of my mind. After all, Ian probably forgot I existed the moment he turned his back.

I wandered around backstage to find my boss, wanting to see if there was anything else for me to do. My job may have seemed insignificant — making sure the right sunglasses were worn on stage — but when it came to rock stars and their image, nothing was insignificant. Working with celebrities meant every move, every act, had to be planned out perfectly.

A few interns stood around watching the band perform. I wished I could take time to watch the show, but I wanted to make a good impression. To be known as a go-getter. I wanted them to offer me a real job. Being a perpetual intern was demoralizing.

I found my boss Janet talking to a man with a staff badge around his neck. Standing a few yards away, I waited until they were done with their conversation. I wanted to pull out my phone and text my sister about my encounter with Ian, but that would have been unprofessional.

It was loud backstage. The music assaulted my ears. It reverberated in my bones. I glanced to the side. If I stood a few more feet to the left, I would have a perfect view of the stage. I debated for long moments. Janet was still busy. I shuffled over, feeling guilty.

Not guilty enough to stop myself.

The drummer was positioned near the back, working the drums at a furious pace. Platinum blond hair, natural, not dyed, flew everywhere with the force of his drumming. His arms were nearly a blur as he pounded away.

"August! Marry me!" One loud fan screamed out during a lull in the music.

His crystal blue eyes were like chips of ice, narrowed in concentration, oblivious to the hollering crowd, paying no attention to the fan calling his name. August Summers concentrated solely on keeping the band in time. I often wondered if he resented his parents for calling him August with a last name like that.

Lead singer Noah Hart stood center stage, gripping the microphone with both hands.

"Noah is a god!" several girls cried at the same time, amplifying their voices.

His burning dark brown eyes narrowed, scorching the audience with passion. He sang with an impressive range, from erotic purrs to rough growling, as if each word were being ripped from his lips. As if his throat was raw and bloody from the pure emotion being wrung out of him.

The crowd was already at a fever pitch, but that didn't stop the bassist from gesturing at the audience to start a mosh pit with a swirl of his hand.

"Come on, you guys!" Cameron shouted out with a manic grin. "It's not a proper show if at least one person doesn't leave with a broken nose!"

His bright, fire-engine red hair glimmered under the spotlights, as if he'd sprinkled glitter over his head. Long strands fell over his face, half covering his heavily kohl-rimmed eyes. The dyed hair should have been damaged and destroyed from all the abuse he put it through, but groupie rumors said it was as soft as a baby's. I snorted at the thought of Cameron Thorne putting his hair though an intense daily conditioning regime.

"Cameron! Take off your shirt!" one girl yelled.

"Yeah, take it off!"

A coordinated chanting started up.

"Take it off, take it off!"

Cameron laughed. "If you insist," he yelled back.

He peeled off his t-shirt to display an exquisitely-toned torso. Squeals and swoons could be heard over the music. I would have been drooling along with the other fangirls, but I'd watched Darkest Days in concert so many times I was immune. Cameron spent most concerts half naked to begin with. Besides, there was someone else I was more interested in.

Ian. Jumping on amps, dropping to his knees, flying across the stage with all the force of a raging inferno. Endless, unstoppable energy.

I was in the wrong spot to get a good look at him, but I could pinpoint the exact moment when two guitars went soaring through the air. The crowd went wild, calling out a single name.

"Da-mi-an! Da-mi-an!"

Two cheeky grins flashed across identical faces, two pairs of green eyes glinted with mirth, as Ian caught Damon's guitar, and Damon caught Ian's.

The Twins had just performed their favorite move: switching guitars in mid-song to play each other's parts.

"Hope? What are you doing standing there?"

Janet spoke to me with an annoyed snap. I cringed. I'd been caught standing around watching the band like the shiftless interns I was trying to one-up.

"I was wondering if you had anything else for me to do." I tried to sound eager and attentive.

"Just keep an eye on all the extra accessories," she said. "We don't want people trying to steal them as souvenirs."

"I'm on it!"

I lugged all the boxes to a corner, found a particularly sturdy one, and sat. No one was going to steal anything on my watch.

Although the concert venue was vast, holding thousands, the backstage was small and cramped. Most of the space was taken up by a row of chairs seated in front of mirrors outlined by lightbulbs. All the acts performing that night had their turn in the chairs on the receiving end of Hair and Makeup.

On the far side a small living room area had been set up, with sofas, armchairs, and coffee tables. This venue didn't have a proper dressing room. That set up would have to do. The lack of dressing rooms meant a large portion of the backstage was curtained off to give the artists privacy when they changed. A few staff members were hovering nearby in case any of the artists had requests before they went on. Most of the crew rushed around with headsets, carrying out their tasks with haste.

The band members never knew how much work went on behind the scenes. They never thought about the personal assistant who handed them their towels. They never thought about the errand boy who had to run out at the last minute to replace bottles of expensive sparkling water.

They never thought about the intern who made sure they had the right sunglasses to wear on stage.

Except one rock star had.

I squirmed, remembering the way Ian had looked at me. Concentrating on my job was difficult with the phantom touch of his thumb brushing my lips.

I closed my eyes and took a slow breath in. I had to cool it or I'd end up a sexually frustrated mess before the night was over. The concert was over six hours long, a collection of artists performing for charity. Darkest Days performed second to last.

I resisted the urge to play with my phone. I was paranoid that would be the moment Janet came to give me more work.

That didn't mean I didn't have something else to occupy my time.

Even though I knew I shouldn't have, even though I told myself to put it out of my mind, I'd strategically placed the boxes so I'd have a good view of the stage from the side.

A perfect view of Ian.

Chapter 3

Ian and his brother stood face to face, hips and guitars canted towards each other. Four deft hands maneuvered wildly across strings for a mid-song guitar duel. The fans screamed until their lungs gave out. The Twins pulled on their whammy bars at the same time and jumped away to opposite sides of the stage with matching smug looks.

Their expressions weren't the only thing that matched. Both heads of light brown hair stood up in soft spikes. Identical leather wrist cuffs covered the backs of their hands and half their forearms. They wore the same band t-shirt, ever changing depending on their current favorite. The Twins would wear an Iron Maiden shirt one week, and a boy band shirt the next. Whether they were serious or not was up in the air, as always.

Their performance was something to behold. The frantic energy they exuded was both exhilarating and exhausting. By the time their set wound down, I felt like I'd been the one jumping and running around on stage.

"Hope!" My manager called. I swung my head forward, pretending I hadn't been watching the concert.

Pretending I hadn't been watching Ian.

"Don't let Damian wander off with those sunglasses or we'll never see them again," Janet said. "We didn't get one of the pairs back last time."

The encore concluded. The band members said their final thanks and farewells. Tomorrow morning Darkest Days would be back in the studio to continue working on their next album.

I stood, ready to intercept. I needed to get those sunglasses back.

August left first, not hanging around to bask in fan adoration. His thin white t-shirt stuck to his chest with sweat, clinging to every peak and valley. Tempting enough for fangirls to swoon over, not that he ever noticed. He took a towel from the outstretched hands of an assistant and handed over his drumsticks without glancing at her, an absentminded look on his face.

Cameron must have run out of souvenirs to throw to the crowd, because he was already tugging Noah off stage with an arm hooked around his neck.

"Would you shove off?" The lead singer gave the bassist a withering glare. His ever-present leather jacket fit his upper body like a glove. Messy black hair fell over his eyes, his brow furrowed in annoyance. Noah shoved an elbow in Cameron's ribs and tried to duck out from under him. Cameron was having none of it.

"Stop your scowling." Cameron tussled with him until Noah gave in. "You were awesome out there tonight. Let me shower you with praise."

Assistants followed behind them like ducklings. Cameron was too busy laughing and trying to jump on Noah's back to notice.

The Twins left the stage last, still pumping their fists to the crowd and raising two fingers in a *rock on* gesture. Their chests heaved as they panted, out of breath from the intense performance. They buzzed with energy, bodies practically vibrating. When they were out of sight of the audience, Ian leaned over and braced himself on his knees, limbs trembling.

Although their eyes were unreadable, hidden behind sunglasses, I saw concern on Damon's face. He placed a firm hand on the back of his brother's neck, bringing their foreheads together. His lips moved, murmuring. Ian shook his head, murmuring back, and got a satisfied nod in return.

The two of them looked back to the audience, still cheering and chanting. The sly expression that crossed both faces was unmistakable. They switched guitars, taking back the instruments they'd each started the concert with.

"I've got your towels, Damian." The assistant who'd previously given them their bottled water was immediately at their sides.

Damon tugged on one of the towels, using it to pull her close. She squeaked as he wrapped an arm around her waist. "You're doing a great job, sweetheart. So attentive to our needs." He whispered something in her ear. She gave him a dazed nod. He kept the arm around her waist as he led her further backstage.

I intercepted, making them halt in front of me. "Sorry, but I need your sunglasses back."

"No problem, sweetness." He tossed them at me with no warning. I fumbled to catch them before they fell. He sidestepped around me, giving me no further thought, all his attention on bottled water girl. She looked to be in a Damian-induced stupor.

Ian was still at the edge of the stage, busy toweling off the sweat from his hair. He didn't see me approach. I took a steadying breath. I wasn't going to let him throw me off balance like before.

"Can I have your sunglasses, Ian?"

He looked up briefly. I could feel him staring at me even through the shades. "One pair wasn't good enough for you?"

My stomach did flips at his teasing smile, but I forced myself not to show it. "My boss wants me to get all the accessories back."

He took off his shades and held them out for me to take. Our hands brushed. It sent a shock from my fingertips, up my arm and through my spine. Every nerve tingled. I yanked my hand back and stuck the shades in my bag for safekeeping.

"Anything else I can give you?" Ian asked. "My shirt? My pants? I'll gladly hand them over. All you have to do is ask."

I swallowed hard. "The sunglasses are fine."

The softly tufted spikes were now a tangled mess falling over his face. I unconsciously reached out and pushed the hair away from his forehead until his green eyes were visible again.

He paused with the towel still in his hand and gave me a puzzled look. I backed away, appalled at myself.

That look turned into a smirk. "Just can't wait to get your hands on me, can you?"

Of course he thought every girl was going to fall for him. It no doubt happened all the time. He probably expected it.

"In your dreams," I shot back.

"Sweetness, you wouldn't be saying that if you knew what kind of dreams I have."

"I'm sure I know exactly what kind of dreams you have, Ian."

That puzzled look was back on his face. He tipped my face up with a finger on my chin, making me look him in the eyes. My insides turned to jelly. Heat radiated from that single point of contact and flowed through my body, centering between my legs.

"Why do you always do that?" he asked.

"Do what?" I said, trying not to let my voice shake at his touch.

"Call me Ian."

I stared at him, confused and aroused at the same time. "Because that's your name...?"

He tilted his head, contemplating. "You're not like the others, are you?" he murmured.

I opened my mouth to respond, but didn't know what to say.

"You should come to our after party," he said, changing the subject.

An after party. With rock stars. Ian invited me to party with him. I was almost giddy at the thought, my mind clouding over. What sort of things did one do at a rock star party?

I remembered bottled water girl and the way she'd succumbed to Damon's attention so easily. I remembered the trail of his fingers along her waist, almost brushing against her ass. I knew exactly what happened at rock star parties.

My heart sped up, but it wasn't only excitement I felt. My body was flooding with nerves.

I told myself to get a grip and took a few steps away. I couldn't think when I was so close to him.

"Sorry, I can't. I've still got work to do. My boss is kind of a hard ass."

Ian blinked at me, taken aback. He started to say something, but before he could speak, the band's manager Naomi called to him.

"August, Damian." She motioned to them with a jerk of her chin.

Ian stared at me for a few long moments, then cracked a grin. "Alright. I'll let you get back to work, sweetheart. Wouldn't want your boss to fire you."

I watched his retreating back for a few moments, then ran my hands over my face, breathing deeply. I needed to get myself under control.

When I looked back up, Naomi had already pulled August and Ian into a discussion. They seemed to be discussing something important.

"We heard back from the music execs," she said. "They want to have another meeting to talk about the concept album."

The drummer nodded, but his gaze drifted back to the stage.

"Where are the others?" Naomi asked, looking around.

Darkest Days' lead singer and bassist were talking with a crew member. Noah frowned and gestured to something behind the stage.

"Cameron, Noah." Naomi called them over.

Cameron grabbed Noah's arm and hauled him away. Noah tugged his arm back, scowl firmly in place. Damon was still off somewhere with bottled water girl. The group put their heads together in a tight circle, conversation inaudible.

I turned my attention away from the band and went back to the boxes. I was supposed to be watching the accessories. Instead, I'd let Ian distract me. I did a quick inventory. Everything was where it was supposed to be.

When I was sure the boxes were untouched, I looked around for a crew member to help me carry them to the car. I turned to find Ian's eyes on me.

He appeared startled for a brief moment, as if he hadn't thought he'd get caught watching me. Long, dark eyelashes swept up and down as he scanned me from hair to toes. Our eyes locked. He winked and the tumbling in my stomach started up again. Even from this distance I could make out the radiant green color, could see the amusement shining in his eyes.

When he finally glanced away, I inhaled deeply and closed my eyes, trying to ignore the shiver running up my spine. I went back to the boxes, distracting myself with work.

But as much as I tried to put it out of my mind, I knew I would never forget the moments when his skin touched mine.

God, I needed to get laid.

Chapter 4

Back at the office the next morning, I made sure all accessories were put back in their places, sunglasses, belts, and all. I took another inventory. Everything matched up with my checklist from the night before. No one stole from Darkest Days with me on the job.

When it was all put away, I tried to sneak out for a break without anyone seeing me. My sister Faith was waiting for me on the first floor near the entrance so we could get lunch together. She called out when she saw me.

"Hey, Hope! You ready?"

"Shh!!" I waved my hands and looked around surreptitiously. "Come on, let's go before anyone notices." I pulled her onto the street.

"What's with the sneaking?" she asked. "Even interns are allowed a lunch break."

I made a face. "The moment I sit down is always when my boss Janet comes looking for me. I've taken to chugging a coffee and cramming a sandwich into my mouth in the women's washroom."

"Let's go to that cafe a few blocks away. It's kind of sketchy. No one ever goes there so your boss won't catch you sitting down."

Faith was right. The place was kind of sketchy, with rickety tables and mismatched chairs, but that just meant the line to order wasn't long. We had our coffee and sandwiches within minutes. I was surprised my sister would set foot into a place like that, but I took one sip of my coffee and understood.

"This coffee is amazing," I said.

"It's pretty good. Better than you can get at most cafes. Still not as good as a traditional french press espresso, though."

"Coffee snob."

"It's called having refined tastes." Faith sipped at her drink, looking at me intently. "I don't want to sound like a bitch, but you look utterly destroyed."

I ran a hand through my hair, smoothing down the flyaway strands. Although we shared the same dark features, with brown eyes and long brown hair, mine was always tangled while hers was smooth and sleek.

"I feel worse than destroyed. I had to be up at five o'clock in the morning yesterday and I worked until nearly dawn. I'm running on empty."

Not to mention, I'd spent the rest of the night thinking about my encounter with Ian.

Faith made a sympathetic noise. She understood my kind of work all too well.

"Enough of my whining. How did your event go?" I asked. I didn't know exactly what she'd been doing the night before, but she was always throwing one corporate event or another.

"It went pretty well. The client was peeved we didn't have sugar free desserts, but all in all it was great."

"Faith, I'm shocked," I said with a fake gasp. "I can't believe you let something slip through the cracks like that."

She made a face at me. "I told my boss about it three weeks ago. She said it wasn't in the budget. Sugar free cupcakes are more expensive." Faith shook her head. "If I was in charge..."

"Give it another six months and you will be." My phoned pinged. "Sorry, I've got to check this. Janet's always messaging me with stuff to do."

"She messages you on your lunch break?"

"She messaged me twenty-four hours a day." I snuck a quick glance. "Never mind, it's just my CHATTR app."

"I thought you weren't the social media type. I can't stand all that stuff."

"Neither can I, but everyone's on it now. It's a good way to keep up with music and fashion industry trends."

Faith laughed at me. "Keeping up to date with industry trends? Really? That's why you're on it?"

"Why else would I be?"

She grabbed at my phone and read aloud. "*Hot new pictures of Damian with up-and-coming runway model. Will The Twins ever settle down?*"

I reached for my phone to grab it back but she held it out of my reach. She continued reading. *"Video of wild Darkest Days' bash proves rock stars really know how to party."*

Faith stared at me. I squirmed.

"Those sure seems like important industry trends," she drawled.

I gave up. "Alright, fine. I set up notifications whenever anyone mentions Darkest Days."

"Of course you did."

"I need to keep tabs on the guys and their music. For my job. You know."

"Right. For your *job*." Faith poked me in the ribs.

"It's not like I follow their every move or anything."

"Of course not."

"I'm a fan but it's not like I'm *obsessed*."

"Mmm-hmm." She sipped her coffee, staring at me over the rim.

I kept digging myself deeper and deeper into the hole. "I just want to know when they release a new song or music video. Or when they announce a new tour or media appearance. Or when one of them changes their hairstyle or has half-naked selfies leaked online."

Faith raised a single eyebrow.

I conceded. "Okay, so maybe I'm a *little* obsessed."

"Well, you wouldn't be the only one. Half the girls on the planet are in love with Darkest Days."

"With good reason. They're rock star gods."

She shrugged. "They've got good songs, I guess."

"You *guess*?"

"You know rock music isn't really my thing." Faith handed me my phone back. "Do you really like getting notifications every time one of those guys trashes a hotel room or bangs another girl?"

I looked down at my coffee, not answering. There was definitely some news I didn't like to get. I hated the idea of Ian sleeping with a bunch of girls. I couldn't pretend it didn't happen, though. The Twins were notorious flirts. They could get any girl they wanted into bed with just a few words.

Faith got tired of teasing me and let me finish my lunch in peace. When we were done she stood up and grabbed her purse.

"I've got to get back to work. Thanks for lunch, Hope. We should do this more often. Even though we live together, I feel like I never get to see you anymore."

"I know. It's not like when we were in school. Having adult careers sucks, doesn't it?"

Faith gave me a squeeze and left. I still had a bit more coffee to finish so I stayed behind. The cafe was empty, leaving me to my thoughts. Ian's words came back to me.

You're not like the others, are you?

I took a sip of my coffee, resisting the urge to flush. I hadn't known what to make of it last night. I still didn't. Ian didn't think I was like the others. Other what? Other girls?

I shook my head and scoffed inwardly. I shouldn't read anything into it. It was probably a line he said to all his female fans.

A jingle announced the cafe door opening. I looked up.

My lungs stopped working.

A tall, gorgeous man with messy brown hair walked in. His eyes were hidden behind sunglasses, but I knew exactly who it was. I sat, frozen, my hands clutching my coffee cup.

Ian didn't see me at first. He ordered a coffee and leaned against the counter, flirting with the barista. "Think you could give me an extra shot of espresso, sweetness?"

She blushed and ducked her head. He tilted her chin up and whispered something in her ear. I couldn't hear what he said, but she squeaked and rushed away. She would no doubt give him exactly what he wanted.

That sounded a lot dirtier in my head than it was meant to.

He scanned the room, waiting. His gaze fell on me. A sly grin crossed his face. The barista came back moments later. He took his coffee without looking at her.

He made his way over to my table. I forced myself to breathe. He would probably walk on by. Of course he wasn't going to remember me. He'd probably flirted with dozens of girls after the concert last night.

Ian stopped in front of my table.

"Mind if I join you?"

Chapter 5

Ian's low, teasing voice did something to my insides. I swallowed hard and couldn't answer. I just stared at him, trying not to melt. He smirked and pulled out the chair.

"What are you doing here, Ian?" The words blurted out without any input from my brain.

He stopped in the middle of sitting down. He tilted his sunglasses down an inch, staring at me over the rim. Those green eyes were penetrating. Every time he looked at me, it turned my insides to mush. This time I felt a spark of something else. It wasn't a flirtatious look. It went deeper. Like he was peeling back my layers and examining my insides. I felt oddly exposed.

"What?" I asked. "Why are you staring at me?"

"How'd you know I wasn't Damon?"

I shrugged. "I can just tell."

"You'd be the first..." he murmured. He pulled the chair over until he was sitting next to me, our knees almost touching. "What's a pretty girl like you doing here? This place is such a dive."

I couldn't think with him that close. I tried to shift away subtly, but he kept on inching forward. "I'm hiding."

"Yeah? Me, too. No one ever comes here, fans or media." He stopped following me and leaned back in his chair, eyeing me up and down. "Who you hiding from?"

It was such a normal question. The kind a fellow intern would ask. Why would a rock star care about the boring details of my day?

"I'm trying to avoid my boss."

"Skipping out on work?" He made a tsk tsk sound. "Naughty girl."

"I needed a break. I've been awake for almost twenty four hours straight."

"Had a wild and crazy night, did you? And they say rock stars party hard."

"I wasn't partying, I was *working,*" I stressed.

"That's no fun. Sounds like you need to let loose a little."

"I'm plenty loose."

Ian laughed. I flushed.

"Shut up, that's not what I meant." I took a flustered sip of my coffee, taking a moment to regain my balance. "And what about you? It's barely past noon. Shouldn't rock stars be nursing their hangovers this early in the day?"

He stretched out his legs, bumping his toe against mine. "Can't get a hangover if you're still drunk."

I debated whether I should shift my foot away or not. Was Ian trying to play footsie with me under the table?

"I thought with your album release date getting closer, Darkest Days would put aside the crazy parties for now."

"You kidding? The closer we get to finishing, the crazier it gets. Gotta work off the steam somehow."

"So you had a fun night partying after the concert, I assume?"

"I would have had a lot more fun if you were there."

I paused with my drink halfway to my mouth. I didn't know if he was being serious or not. I thought back to the notification about *Damian* and a model. It hadn't said which twin they were talking about. It could have been Ian, or it could have been his brother Damon.

In either case, it didn't matter. Everyone knew The Twins could get any girl they wanted. I wasn't anyone special.

"I'm sure you managed to have all sorts of fun without me."

"Sweetness, you have no idea what kind of fun I can get up to." He pushed his sunglasses to the top of his head and gave me a wicked grin. "Maybe next time I can show you. Would you like that?"

I breathed shallow breaths, not wanting him to know how fast my heart was racing. "If you're going to make innuendos at me, you could at least call me by my name."

"Which is?"

"Hope."

He snickered and leaned forward in his chair, eyes sparkling. "That's adorable."

I wrinkled my nose in distaste. "I hate it. It sounds all virtuous and pure. "

"Nothing wrong with virtuous."

"That's rich, coming from a guy like you."

"I don't mind the innocent type. Makes it so much more fun to corrupt them."

I couldn't stop the flush of heat that rushed through my body, heading straight between my legs. I knew exactly how he corrupted the innocent.

My phone pinged. Ian raised an eyebrow as I reached for it.

"Sorry, I know this is rude, but I have to check it. My boss is always giving me more stuff to do." I pulled out my phone.

One text from my sister. *Thanks for the lunch. Hope your boss isn't too much of a dick today.*

"Your boss?" Ian asked.

"No, it's my sister, Faith."

"Hope and Faith? Really?"

"So original, I know. She's always asking how my internship is going," I put my phone back in my pocket.

"And how is it going?"

"It's great. I lug boxes and guard accessories."

"So rock star life is treating you well, then?" Ian teased.

"I guess. It's just..."

"What?"

I hesitated before answering. Did Ian actually care about my answer or was he just looking for another way to needle me?

"I'm a box carrier. Sunglasses fetcher. I'd wanted an internship where I'd be more than coffee maker and errand girl. I'd thought this would be it."

Ian nodded in understanding. "The entertainment industry isn't all glamour and glory like everyone thinks. It was eye opening to see all the grunt work that goes on behind the scenes."

I eyed him, surprised at the comment. "It always kind of annoyed me, actually, that you guys never seem to realize how many people wait on you hand and foot."

The corner of Ian's lips tilted up. "You believe that old stereotype about celebrities ignoring the little people once we get famous?"

"No! I mean, I understand. You have your own jobs to do. Important jobs. You can't be thinking about every menial staff member who helps your careers run like well-oiled machines."

"I'm sure what you do isn't menial."

"Box carrier and sunglasses fetcher, remember? It certainly isn't as important as your job." I leaned back into my chair with a groan. "I know I shouldn't complain. I'm lucky to have an internship at all, let alone one at Etude Entertainment, considering how much competition is out there."

"So modest." He smirked. "I'm sure it wasn't just luck."

"It's not modesty. I know I got lucky. I have friends who also applied, people much more competent than me. I would have been happy for them if they'd been chosen instead."

He trailed one finger through the dark hair framing my face. "Such a sweet girl, aren't you?" My breath hitched. "Are you just as sweet everywhere else?" he murmured, low enough so only I could hear. A flood of warmth hit my gut like a tsunami, then continued downward, centering between my legs.

I swallowed hard and took deep breaths. I needed to get myself under control.

Ian gave me a teasing grin and continued talking as if he hadn't just nearly made me orgasm through words alone.

"I know the feeling. Before August found me and my brother, we were playing..."

He stopped sharply. I blinked at the sudden pause, but he continued speaking seconds later.

"...in this shitty little garage band, going absolutely nowhere. Then here comes August Summers, saying he wants us in his band. I thought I'd fucking died on the spot."

"You've certainly come a long way from a shitty garage band."

"You sound jealous." Ian's eyes sparkled with humor as he leaned forward. "You had dreams of being a rock star when you were a little girl?"

I scooted back in my seat. I couldn't be that close to him without turning into goo.

"No. I'm just really low on the totem pole right now. The lowest possible. I'd hoped by now I'd have a real career, but that doesn't seem to be happening."

I rambled, not thinking about what I was saying before the words left my mouth. Being near Ian was like something flipping the *off* switch for my brain.

"I hate going from one internship to another without any real job offers. I keep calling myself a perpetual intern. It's demoralizing. My sister Faith was never—"

I cut myself off, not wanting to wallow in self pity in front of Ian.

But he just tilted his head, waiting for me to continue. As if he was genuinely interested.

For some reason, I wanted to tell him. I wanted to tell him all the feelings I'd been suppressing. The look on his face was understanding. Encouraging.

"My sister got hired at an event company right out of school," I blurted out. "She's already been promoted twice. Faith is blasé about her success and never rubs it in, but I can't help feel inadequate next to her. Event Logistics Specialist sounds so much better than *intern*."

"You feel jealous?"

"I love my sister. I want nothing but the best for her."

"But...?"

I fiddled with my coffee cup. "I just wish I could be as good at something as she is," I confessed quietly. "That I could be as successful as her."

"Hope, you scored an internship at one of the most sought-after companies in the country. Only a handful of people who apply get one. That in itself is impressive."

I gave him a small smile. "The rock star is telling the intern she's impressive? Are you trying to flatter me?"

"Just making an observation." Ian said, parroting the words I'd told him back at me.

I sat up in my seat. "I'm not trying to wallow in self pity. I've got a plan. I'm going to work my way up. If I work hard enough, eventually someone will notice me."

He smirked. "Someone already has."

I flushed, heartbeat speeding up. "I meant someone important."

Ian threw his head back, faking a pained groan. "Shit, you know how to hurt a guy's ego, don't you?"

"No! That's not what I meant. I was talking about one of my bosses. Someone who could hire me for real."

He examined me closely, thinking for a moment. "I could put in a good word for you."

"You would do that?"

"It's like I said last night. Wouldn't want to lose such a pretty face."

My breath caught. I reminded myself it didn't mean anything. He and his brother probably said it to all the girls. "Um. No thanks. I don't want special treatment. I don't want people thinking you're doing a favor for one of your groupies."

"Sweetheart, with the way you've been shutting me down, no one's going to think you're a groupie."

I was melting under his gaze. If that was what he called *shutting him down,* I'd hate to see what it looked like when a girl fell under his spell. Then again, bottled water girl had floated off into the clouds when Damon pulled her aside after the concert.

"Ian, with The Twins' reputation, anyone who sees me talking to you is going to think I'm just another groupie."

He looked away. "Can't argue with that," he murmured. His expression turned dark for a brief moment, lips turning down into a frown. I wondered why. Surely he knew better than anyone the rumors about *Damian* and their behavior towards women.

"Not that I don't appreciate the offer," I continued. "I just don't want any favoritism."

"I get it. You want to prove you can do it on your own. Very noble." He grinned, all signs of his earlier frown having disappeared. "It's almost... virtuous."

"Funny."

"Just saying. Everybody uses their connections to get ahead in this industry. It's nothing to be ashamed of."

"Yes it is. Can't you understand how mortifying it would be if a famous rock star told my boss to give me a job? Everyone would think—" I cut myself off, flushing.

Ian smirked. "Go on. What would people think?"

I stared into my coffee, avoiding his gaze. "You know exactly what they'd think."

"Maybe I don't. Tell me."

"They'd think that we..." I trailed off, squirming.

Ian leaned forward until our thighs pressed together. He trailed his finger along my jaw. I looked up with a start. "That we what?"

My inner muscles clenched from that touch. The urge to lean into it was as strong as the urge to run away. "You already know."

"Maybe I just want to hear you say it."

My stomach leaped into my throat. I could barely think through the haze of desire clouding my mind.

Then the curve of his smile turned into a wicked smirk and the fog lifted. My brain snapped back in a fit of pique.

He was playing me just like he played with all his fans.

I looked him dead in the eyes. "I'm not going to speculate on our hypothetical sex life in public, so you might as well give up."

Ian's eyes grew wide and stunned for a brief moment. He sat back in his chair, chuckling. "You're something else, sweetheart."

My heart was still pumping madly. "Gee, thanks."

"That's a good thing," he clarified. "Besides, I get it. I had to work my way up, too. I didn't get any special treatment. Damon and I went through hell to get where we are." Ian's eyes widened, looking almost startled with himself. He cleared his throat and leaned back in his chair, a deceptively casual gesture. Maybe he hadn't meant to say that. "I just mean, I understand where you're coming from," he continued, recovering smoothly.

I wanted to ask him about it. What kind of hell had he gone through? Maybe we had more in common than I thought.

I snorted inwardly at myself. What could I possibly have in common with a famous rock star playboy like Ian?

Still, talking to him about this kind of stuff was... nice. It was different. He wasn't just teasing me. We were talking to each other like two regular people. "I know a lot about how Darkest Days was formed, but there's not much info online about you guys before the band." I left the question unspoken.

He looked uncomfortable, shifting in his chair. He was silent for long moments before chugging down the rest of his coffee, avoiding my eyes. "Sorry sweetness, gotta go."

I tried not to look disappointed. "I guess I should be getting back, too. I've got work to do."

"And a rock star's work is never done."

"I suppose you've got fans to seduce and hotel rooms to trash."

"Something like that." Ian gave me one last unreadable look. He leaned forward slowly. I froze. He angled his head, as if aiming for a kiss. My eyelids fluttered closed unconsciously as I held my breath.

Soft lips touched skin.

My eyes flew open in surprise as Ian kissed me on the tip of my nose. He laughed as I jolted back and rubbed at my nose with the back of my hand. "What the hell was that?"

"You're too cute." His gaze held a sort of predatory glimmer. "I think I'm going to have fun with you."

My stomach fluttered. I ducked my head, trying to hide the flush on my face. There was something about Ian that knocked me off balance. I didn't know if I liked it, but I couldn't deny my attraction.

He flipped his shades back down over his eyes. "See you around, sweetheart. Let's do another coffee date again sometime."

I was still reeling from the almost-kiss when the cafe door jingled, signaling his exit.

My hands trembled as I gripped my coffee cup. How was it possible a kiss on the nose could affect me so much?

It wasn't just that brief touch of his lips, though. It was Ian. Just Ian.

He's a flirt, I reminded myself. *He has this effect on everyone. It doesn't mean anything.*

My body disagreed. It was telling me this meant *everything.*

My heart, on the other hand, was sending warning signals.

Don't even start, it screeched. *You know what guys like him are like.*

I did. I knew exactly how Ian's type operated. They said whatever they needed to ensnare you. They used all their charm, all their tricks. Then once they had you, they threw it all away.

I didn't want to let myself get played for a fool again.

But I couldn't stop remembering the look in Ian's eyes every time I called him by name.

Chapter 6

After my lunch break — after my surprise *coffee date* with Ian — I went back to work.

Or, it would be more accurate to say, I *tried* to go back to work. I was thoroughly distracted by the thought of a certain flirtatious rock star.

I knew he acted like that with all the girls. I *knew* that.

But the more we had talked, the less he had overtly flirted with me. He'd started to touch on something about his past before stopping. Something personal. And I'd confessed something I'd never told anyone — my jealousy of Faith, and my angst about my nonexistent career.

I couldn't help thinking maybe there could be something deeper between us.

My phone pinged, startling me out of my thoughts. My CHATTR app again. I scrolled through the newsfeed quickly. It was just the usual fangirl squealing and music reviewer snarking.

Wait.

I tapped an article shared by a popular music reviewer. I skimmed it briefly and scrolled until I found a gallery of photos. My heart sank. This wasn't good. Not for Darkest Days, and not for Etude.

Then an idea came to me in one burst. My mind raced, ideas considered and discarded within split seconds. I could practically hear the whirring sound of my brain working overtime. One complete, perfect idea solidified into shape. I could almost *see* it.

I'd just figured out how to get my bosses to notice me.

I made my way through the hallways at Etude, my mind going a million miles an hour. I knew Janet was scheduled to be in a meeting on the seventeenth floor. I found her in a conference room, setting up her laptop to project on a blank screen.

"Janet, do you have a second?"

She pointedly glanced up at the wall clock. "I have a meeting in five minutes."

"This won't take long."

She crossed her arms. I hurried to speak.

"When I first started here, I was told the band was working on a concept album. I've heard some of the songs and they have to do with sex and love."

"Yes, that's right." Janet sounded irritated, but I pressed on.

"I think there may be a problem."

She huffed out an impatient sigh. "Yes?"

"There's another band doing the same concept," I rushed out. "I was researching trends in fashion and music." Yeah, let's go with that excuse. "The rock band Feral Silence came out with a new album. The themes are very similar."

Her expression turned no-nonsense. "Explain."

"Their album has to do with types of relationships. First love, casual sex, soulmates, that kind of thing."

A crease appeared between her brows. "That *is* similar."

"Everyone knows Darkest Days and Feral Silence are rivals. If they put out an album with the same theme, people will think they're copying."

The worried look on Janet's face told me she thought the same. "The marketing team won't like this. But there's no way August will change his vision. He's too stubborn."

"I was thinking. What if the theme was similar but the concept was different?"

"Themes and concepts are the same thing."

"Not always. I had an idea."

She scoffed. "It's not up to an intern to second guess the artist, Hope."

"But I think it could work," I insisted. Janet frowned at me and I hurried to get my idea in before she shut me down. "The concept should be the rise and fall of a relationship."

48

"Yes, well, thank you for your input, Hope, but I think—"

She was interrupted when a voice spoke up from behind me.

"Tell me more."

My heart jumped as I whirled around. The members of Darkest Days stood outside the door.

August, founder of the band, main composer, producer, and universally acknowledged musical genius, stared at me with piercing eyes. I gulped under that intense gaze.

Should I be flattered or nervous?

I flicked my eyes to the rest of the band. Noah's expression was aloof as always, but Cameron's interest was piqued.

Ian and Damon both had a playful quirk to their lips. The Twins wore dark sunglasses, but Ian's face brightened up when he saw me. Damon looked slightly annoyed. The difference was almost imperceptible.

The memory of Ian's almost-kiss nearly made me whimper. I coughed to cover it.

"You said you had a new idea for our concept?" August prompted.

I fought to make my voice work. After a shaky start, I made myself coherent.

"I don't know how much you heard, but Feral Silence's new album has themes similar to yours. I know your songs are set in stone, but the concept we use for the marketing can be re-worked. Instead of sex and love, the theme could be the rise and fall of a relationship. From early love to passionate conflict and painful parting to bitter heartbreak. Each member of the band can represent one stage of the relationship."

"How'd you come up with that?" Cameron's eyes sparkled with enthusiasm. At least one member of the band liked my idea.

"I thought about the meaning of the album, and the feelings you were trying to put into the songs. When I tried to come up with how each band member might fit into that, it came to me all at once."

"You only gave four stages," Ian and Damon said at the same time. "There's five of us." They tilted their heads in unison.

"You two are both the conflict stage. One is the passionate fighting, one is the—" I cleared my throat and tried not to stutter, "—the passionate makeup sex. Like a yin-yang sort of thing."

"And which one is which?" they both said.

I nearly blushed at Ian's seductive smirk. Before I could answer, Janet interrupted.

"Thank you very much for your input, Hope, but that's enough wasting time. We have a meeting in a few minutes."

They weren't going to listen to my idea. I wanted to melt into an embarrassed puddle on the floor. I also wanted to throw my hands up in frustration.

"I like it."

I blinked at August in surprise.

"Do you always keep this up to date on industry trends?" he asked.

"I try to."

"Hope is an intern in the Product Development department," Janet said dismissively.

"I've got a degree in Fine Arts," I blurted out. I regretted it the moment the words left my lips. They wouldn't care what I went to school for.

"An artist, huh?" Ian said.

"You the creative type?" Damon continued.

"Spend your days painting masterpieces?"

"Gonna be the next Picasso?"

"Should we be getting your autograph?"

"Um. No. I just make sure your clothes aren't wrinkled before you go on stage."

They both snickered.

"Damian. What do you think?" August asked, inclining his head towards me.

The Twins gave me considering looks. They both shared a quick glance at each other, communicating without words.

"We say yes." They both spoke at the same time.

"Cameron? Noah?"

"Why the hell not?" Cameron grinned.

"Whatever," Noah muttered.

"Alright. I think we're done here." August said

"Yes, let's move on and get the meeting started," Janet said briskly.

My insides went cold. They were going to just dismiss me.

August shook his head. "I meant I'm calling off the meeting. There's nothing to discuss anymore." He looked me up and down, a considering stare. He nodded once to himself.

"We found our Image Consultant."

I froze, my mind going blank. I couldn't comprehend the words coming out of August's mouth. "What?"

"Your idea is brilliant," August continued. "The exact kind of thinking we need."

Janet opened her mouth to speak as if to interrupt, but August spoke right over her.

"This new album is going to be a great undertaking. Every ad, every photoshoot, every music video, needs to convey the right feeling. The right image. We need someone to work on our promotional campaign to make sure everything is consistent. To make sure our concept is conveyed in everything we do."

"Like a continuity editor." Ian said.

"I don't know what that means," I confessed.

"It's like when you're producing a TV show," he explained. "Or movie. If the actor is wearing blue jeans and white sneakers when the director calls cut for the day, the continuity editor makes sure they're wearing the same thing when they pick up filming three days later."

"That's only half of it," August said. "We don't just need someone to oversee everything. We need someone creative. We need someone who can take the feelings and meanings of our songs and bring them to life. Someone who can bring our metaphorical ideals into the physical world. Someone who can reduce a concept to visual icons. We need an Image Consultant."

"We need a miracle worker," Noah interjected with a mutter and a snort.

They needed a miracle worker, alright. Taking metaphors and making them physical? My mouth went dry. There was no way I could do something like that.

Was there?

"Shouldn't the marketing department have people to do all that?" I asked. "Wardrobe Stylists and Branding Specialists or whatever."

"They're overworked dealing with all of Etude's other artists," Cameron replied. "We can rely on them to help, but we need one person concentrating solely on our album release."

"And I want that person to be you," August added.

Image Consultant. Me. Darkest Days, one of the hottest rock bands to debut in years, wanted some nobody intern to work with them to develop their image and brand for their new album. It was too overwhelming. Some part of me wanted to object and turn them down on the spot.

But another part of me started to buzz with excitement. Taking the thoughts and feelings of rock stars and making them real? I would have to use all my artistic skills. It would force me to stretch my abilities to the breaking point. If I pulled it off, I could say I helped create one of the most successful, most creative, album releases in years.

Ian pushed his sunglasses up until they rested on the top of his head. He scanned me up and down slowly, undressing me with his eyes. That carnal stare, that wicked grin, told me his mind was filling with dirty thoughts.

The lump of fear and worry in my gut melted away, something else taking its place. Something hot. Something hungry. The look in Ian's eyes was unlocking something deep inside me. I wanted to know exactly what sort of dirty things he was thinking. I wanted him to tell me. To show me.

As long as I kept my heart guarded against his charm, surely there was no harm in letting him flirt with me. And perhaps more.

"It sounds like a challenge."

If I took this job, maybe I'd get the chance.

"I'm in."

Chapter 7

As a Darkest Days fan, sitting in on a jam session was a dream come true. I was allowed to watch the band practice their songs a few more times before recording a final version. *For inspiration,* August had said.

It was infinitely better than seeing them perform on stage. During a concert you were stuck behind a barrier lined with bodyguards. You were lucky if you got close enough to see their faces and were forced to listen through booming, staticky speakers.

Watching the guys sing and play in person was breathtaking. It was so raw, so *real.* They didn't need to put on their rock star personas to win over fans. They could be themselves.

I quickly learned what *being themselves* actually meant. They didn't have to act like bad ass sex gods. They were a bunch of rowdy, twenty-something boys playing around and making music with their friends.

Ian and Damon were nearly uncontrollable. They wouldn't sit still, dashing from one corner of the room to the other, jumping up on tables and kicking over chairs with bursts of laughter.

They finished one particularly intense and awe-inspiring dueling guitar solo, then lifted their instruments high above their heads, as if prepared to swing them down.

"No— Wait—!" several assistants cried, not wanting The Twins to smash up another pair of guitars.

They snickered and lowered the instruments, giving each other a fist bump.

"Damian, chill the fuck out and play your goddamn instruments."

August spoke the admonishing words with a slight smile, so I knew he wasn't angry with them. Mildly annoyed, perhaps, but indulgent in the way a parent would be.

"You're supposed to be professionals. Gifted with ungodly talent. Stop acting like three year olds hopped up on sugar."

"Where's the fun in that?" They both said at the same time, grinning.

I was surprised to see August much more animated than usual. Of course, that was because he had to act the tyrant and herd the other band members.

It made me wonder how old August was. Aside from Cameron and his sometimes-baby face, August looked the youngest, but acted like the oldest. Being a universally acknowledged musical genius probably matured a person.

Noah sang with a fiery passion, growling low in his chest. In the quiet moments between words his eyebrows drew down into a frown. The lead singer was wound up, muscles tense with a scowl on his face. Then the lyrics picked up again and he let loose, switching between erotic crooning and despondent wailing. Noah didn't look upset at anything in particular — except when Cameron started bugging him.

"You keep frowning like a grumpy old man, your face is gonna to stay like that," Cameron said in a mocking tone.

Noah glared at Cameron, who just laughed and looked down at his bass guitar, pretending to focus on the music. Noah's dark expression should have been disconcerting. Instead, it was oddly endearing. Like a kitten with his fur puffed up.

I made sure to keep that thought to myself. I was sure Noah would murder me if he knew I compared him to an angry kitten.

There were a handful of other interns attending the recording sessions, mostly from social media and public relations, taking candid behind-the-scenes photos and videos of the band for promotional material.

Whoever hired the interns didn't do a good job weeding out the obsessive fangirls. They giggled and blushed, cooing at whomever paid them the most attention.

I sat in a corner as far away from the action as I could, not wanting to be a disturbance. I was there to get a better feel for their music, to help my creative process.

I shouldn't have bothered. Ian's eyes were constantly on mine, always flicking to me in the quiet moments between his antics. He would throw me an irresistible look, eyes twinkling with sinful glee, and make provocative innuendos meant only for me.

I ignored him as best as I could, not wanting to encourage him. The interns pouted and glared at me whenever Ian made a comment and doubled their efforts to gain his attention. The last thing I needed was jealous colleagues.

The other band members paid it no mind, clearly used to Ian's flirtations. Except for Damon. Whenever he noticed Ian's teasing and my flushed cheeks, his lips twisted in a mildly disgruntled expression. I wondered why. Was it because I was only showing interest in his brother? Clearly most other girls, especially fans and groupies, didn't care whether they snagged Damon or Ian. Either one of The Twins was good enough. Was Damon jealous I wasn't interested in him, too?

Too bad. Damon would have to learn not all girls would fall over themselves to be around him.

Of course, I doubted he would learn that lesson today. Whenever the girls sidled up next to Ian he gave them teasing smiles but didn't engage in his usual excessive flirting. The disappointment on their faces only lasted as long as it took for them to turn their attention to Ian's brother instead. Damon, of course, basked in their adoration. He reached out to stroke their hair and whispered things in their ears that made them blush. Clearly, it didn't matter to them which half of *Damian* flirted with them.

Not all of them acted like that, though. At least a handful were there to do their actual jobs.

"Damian!" One of the PR girls held up her phone in a questioning gesture. "Can you guys pose next to each other with your guitars?"

They both reveled in the attention, throwing their arms over each other's shoulders and facing the girl.

She pursed her lips. "No, that's not quite right. Can you both move your feet so you're in the same position? And you're not holding your guitars the same way. Can you mimic each other's fingers on the fret board?"

They both complied, shuffling their limbs. The girl raised her phone to her face, then lowered it with a shake of her head.

"It's still not symmetrical. I need you guys to be posed the exact same."

Ian stiffened minutely, his lightly amused expression frozen on his face. Damon hugged his twin with a squeeze around his shoulder.

"Got it," Damon said. "One person, two bodies, right?"

"Exactly."

Ian's expression grew dark for a brief moment. I sat up in my chair, worried. Then his face smoothed out, mirroring his twin's and shifting his body. "Does this work for you?"

"Perfect!" The girl snapped picture after picture, but was quick about it, only taking up ten seconds of their time. She moved on to the next one. "Noah! Give me a sexy glare."

Noah jerked in surprise, his usual glower softening. The girl shook her head.

"No, not that look. The other one. Like you're pissed off."

Cameron immediately flung himself at Noah, clinging to him and ruffling his hair. "This'll get him all worked up."

"Get the fuck off," Noah grumbled, elbowing Cameron in the ribs.

The bassist laughed and bounced away. "There you go babe, one pissed off look."

The camera snapped a dozen times. Noah glared at Cameron's retreating back.

"Perfect! August, you're next."

Ian detangled himself from his brother, his expression clouded again. He murmured something into Damon's ear, nodding his head towards the door. He lifted his arms up high, stretching as he walked out of the room. The motion made his t-shirt ride up, exposing a stripe of toned abs and a line of dusky hair leading to...

My heart beat faster. I glanced away, not wanting to get caught staring.

I continued taking notes as the social media and PR people took their pictures and asked their questions. Watching the band members interact with each other in such a casual setting was eye opening. My brain was nearly bursting with ideas.

The band set up to start another song. Ian was still gone.

"Hey guys, hold up a minute," Damon said.

"Where's your bro?" Cameron asked.

"Went to get a coffee. Said he needed a breather."

"Why don't we all take twenty?" August suggested. "We've been at this for a while."

"I'll go find him and let him know there's no rush," Damon said.

"No, let me." I jumped up without thinking. "I, uh, I need a coffee, too. I'm sure I'll run into him."

August nodded. Noah didn't even acknowledge I was alive. Cameron, on the other hand, gave me a smirk so wide it was alarming. And Damon...

Damon was trying to set me on fire with his eyes alone.

Chapter 8

Alarmed at the look Damon gave me, I quickly glanced away and scurried out with a mumbled excuse.

I didn't want a coffee. I wanted to find Ian by myself. I was worried about him. He'd been upset when he left, and I didn't think anyone else had noticed.

Ian wasn't waiting in line at the coffee shop on the first floor of the building. I didn't think he'd have enough time to go across the street to the cafe. I gave up and made my way back up to the practice studio, feeling dejected.

I was relieved to step out of the elevator and run into him on his way back.

"Hey! I was looking for you."

I expected him to crack a joke, insinuating I was looking for him for naughty reasons. Instead he appeared startled, eyes wide and glassy.

"H-hey," he stammered. He clutched at his wrist cuff, playing with the buckles again. There was a small patch of white sticking out from underneath. Like gauze. I was immediately concerned. I reached for his wrist.

"Did you hurt yourself?"

He pulled back with a jolt. I blinked, confused.

"No, I—" he paused for a moment, gathering himself together. "Just a scratch. The maintenance guys should fix those hand dryers in the men's washroom. They're all sharp edges."

I glanced back down as he continued fiddling with his wrist. "You sure it's just a scratch?"

"Nothing to worry about." He eyed me up and down slowly. "Did I tell you, you look absolutely delicious today?"

My heart sped up at the hunger in his eyes, all thoughts of injuries forgotten. "You might have mentioned it once or twice in front of everyone."

"Only once or twice? I'll have to do better next time."

"I'm sure your horde of fangirls will just love that."

"You seem to have a problem with jealousy."

"No, I don't!"

"You do. It's cute."

"Whatever. It's not like I care. Go ahead and flirt with whomever you like."

He gave me a teasing smile. "Maybe I'll leave the flirting up to Damon from now on, if it makes you so jealous."

"And let down all your fans? You would never."

"It's not like girls care which twin is doing the flirting."

"Why do you think that?"

He gave a rueful laugh. "Didn't you hear? One person, two bodies. We're the exact same. No difference between us."

"There is, though. I know everyone thinks you and Damon are identical, but you're not."

"And what exactly makes me different from my brother?" He leaned into me, encroaching on my personal space, inches away from me.

"I think—" I could smell him. Something strong and hot, like smoke and spice. It sent my head spinning. That was the only reason I answered the way I did.

"I think there's something different about you. Something smoldering inside. Damon is ferocious like a wildfire. Out of control. You're different from your brother. You're more of a slow burn. You scorch people from the inside out. Turn people to ash before they notice you've burned them, and when they do, they don't care. Your fans love it. Your fans want it."

"Fans?" He trailed the back of one finger along my cheek, from temple to jaw. "Or you?"

"Ah—" All I could make was the tiniest of sounds. Nothing else would leave my lips.

He continued down my throat, until he reached the gap in my shirt covering the swell of my breasts. I tensed up. I didn't know if I should ask him to stop or beg him to continue. Instead of moving lower, he cupped my face with both hands and raised my head up.

"How else am I different?"

I parted my lips, not knowing how to continue.

"Tell me," he insisted.

"You're more intense," I blurted out. "Damon only looks at the surface. With you, it's like you're seeing something deeper." I glanced away, embarrassed, and tried to think of something less personal I could tell him. "You're less rash. Damon jumps in without thinking. You're more thoughtful."

I went quiet, not knowing how much more I should say. I didn't want him to think I was some sort of stalker who watched him every minute of the day, who dissected his every move, his every word.

Even though I sort of was.

"You really think all that?" Ian's voice was soft, quiet. I glanced back up at him. His eyes flicked from left to right, as if they were searching mine.

"Yes. I really think all that."

He stared at me silently for several long moments.

With no warning, he captured my lips in a crushing kiss. I almost jerked back in surprise, but I didn't dare move away.

Ian was kissing me. The thought made my head swim. The hair on the back of my neck stood up, every nerve ending on fire.

If I expected soft kisses and romance, I would have been mistaken. Ian forced my lips open with his tongue, assaulting my mouth with fervent heat. I let out a soft moan. It only urged him on. I clutched his shoulders to keep my balance. The force of his kiss made me lightheaded. I was afraid my legs would fall out from under me.

He must have noticed. Ian pulled me closer, wrapping both arms around my waist, keeping me upright. He tugged me until his hips were angled into mine, tight against him.

"God, I love your mouth," he murmured against my lips. "Such a sweet girl."

I froze. Ian and the L word in the same sentence? My heart couldn't handle it.

As he continued kissing me, I slowly relaxed. I knew this meant nothing to him. I knew I was his newest plaything. I could accept that. That was all I wanted from him, anyway.

The kiss slowed. He stroked his tongue against mine. They slid together softly. Each flick of his tongue sent sparks shooting through my spine. He bit lightly on my lower lip. I let out a soft sound in the back of my throat. The taste of him, the smell of him, was driving me crazy.

Warm and spicy.

It was innately *masculine*.

After several long minutes, I finally had to break away for air. He continued the kisses, sliding his lips to my neck, leaving a blazing hot trail. He applied a soft suction and I nearly whimpered out loud. Then he bit down and I couldn't stop a gasp from escaping, bucking my hips against his in surprise.

He returned to my mouth, tangling his tongue with mine, his lips pulling moans and whimpers out of me.

I jolted back at the press of one hand against my bare stomach. My shirt had come untucked from my skirt. Ian took advantage, sliding one hand up until fingers brushed the edge of my bra. He stopped. Waiting for my permission? I couldn't speak. I didn't want to tear my lips away from his. Instead I arched my back, pushing into his hands.

He accepted the invitation, cupping one breast in a gentle hand. Through thin cotton a thumb rubbed idly back and forth across my nipple. That motion sent a wave of heat soaring through my body. My insides clenched. The ache between my legs grew stronger. My panties were getting damp.

He must have felt the shudder running through me. One knee found its way between my legs, hiking my skirt around my waist. The press of his thigh against my very center caused my brain to fizzle out. My hips rocked unconsciously, trying to get more friction.

Heavy footsteps echoed down the hallway.

I pulled away with a gasp, pushing at Ian's chest. He barely moved an inch.

"What—"

I cut him off with a sharp hiss.

"Someone's coming."

I quickly pulled my skirt into place, attempting to tuck in my shirt with one hand while smoothing my hair with the other.

"What are you doing here?" Damon popped around the corner a few seconds later. "August wants us all together. Right now."

"Be there in a minute." Ian didn't take his eyes off me. I flushed and took a few more steps back.

"Whatever, man," Damon snorted and left.

Ian and I stood in silence for a few moments. I was still catching my breath, but he was unruffled. How often did he accost unsuspecting interns in the middle of the work day? He must have sensed I was still reeling. He moved back a few paces.

"Why did you kiss me?" I asked, my breathing still uneven.

"Because I wanted to." He smirked. "Are you telling me you didn't like it? Because I'd like to do a whole lot more than kissing."

I bit my lip and forced myself to answer truthfully. "No. I liked it."

His lips quirked up as a smug look spread across his face. "There's a party tonight."

I blinked at the non sequitur. "What?"

"Cam's throwing a huge party at his place. You should come."

"You're inviting me to another party?"

"This one's gonna be a rager." His eyes were alight with mischief. "There will be a bodyguard checking the guest list. Give them your name and tell them Damian invited you." He gave me a wink and sauntered off to join his bandmates. My lips still tingled.

"Wait!" I called. He tilted his head, questioning. "I'd rather tell them Ian invited me."

His eyes widened slightly, that same expression of wonder I'd seen before. His lips turned down slightly before cracking a small, rueful smile. "You can try, sweetheart." He flipped his sunglasses down over his eyes, hiding that brilliant green. "But I doubt they'll know who you mean."

Chapter 9

I almost didn't make it to the party. Not because I was nervous or had second thoughts. I almost didn't make it because of Janet.

"Please please *please*," I begged Faith as she rifled through her closet. "I know it's inconvenient, but my boss asked for these documents tonight because she has an early morning meeting and she wants me to drop them off right now, but I need to get ready for the party and *please* can you deliver them?"

Faith finally gave in. "Ugh. Fine. Stop begging. I'll do it. You just remember this the next time my boss asks me to do three things at once."

"I''ll be the errand girl next time, I promise."

She took a dress out of the back of her closet and threw it at me. "Here. Try this on. There's no way I'm letting you leave the house in your usual leggings and baggy sweaters."

"Interesting choice." The high neckline and long sleeves surprised me. She never wore anything scandalous, but Faith's style was less stuffy than the outfit suggested.

"It's called *seven dresses in one.*" She pulled one of the arms out of the sleeve and did some complicated folding, turning it into a fashionable one sleeve dress with a just-barely-decent scooped neck. She also shifted the fabric around my waist to raise the hemline.

"I know I always say you should get out of the house more, but are you sure you want to party with rock stars?" Faith's voice was laced with concern. "Those things can get kind of crazy."

I hadn't told my sister the invitation had come from Ian personally. I didn't want her to start getting thoughts about me and him.

Even though she wouldn't have been wrong.

"I really want to go. I think it's important. For networking. Getting to know my colleagues. That kind of thing."

It wasn't a complete lie. I *would* be getting to know my colleagues. Just not the way Faith imagined.

Ian had kissed me. He'd more than kissed me. We made out at work where anyone could have caught us. Damon almost did catch us. I swallowed hard. The butterflies in my stomach were taking wing from the most fleeting of memories.

And now Ian had invited me to a house party with him and his bandmates.

The thought gave me shivers, fear and excitement both taking hold. I didn't want to be *that* girl. The one who threw herself at rock stars. I didn't want Ian to think I was some sort of groupie. I didn't want him to think I was only interested in him because he was famous.

There was something about Ian that intrigued me. Even if he wasn't a rock star, I would have been interested in him.

The question was, was Ian interested in me for real, or did he see me as another plaything?

And if he did... would that really be so bad? Wasn't that what I wanted?

There was a chasm within me and it felt like I was teetering on the edge.

I didn't want to be just another girl in Ian's long line of conquests.

I didn't want to risk opening my heart only for him to throw it away.

Those thoughts kept running through my head during the taxi ride to Cameron's place. I came to a stop in front of a mansion in one of the wealthier parts of town. Star athletes and other celebrities also lived on this street.

Cameron owned a house *here*?

How much money did rock stars make?

A crowd of dozens milled around the front steps. Taking a deep breath, I opened the car door. As nervous as I was, I didn't want to show it. I was going to play it cool. I was going to be classy and sophisticated like my sister.

I wasn't going to act like the complete wreck I felt inside.

Lights flashed bright and hot, burning my retinas. The clicking sound of camera shutters assaulted my ears. People called out questions, but there were so many voices I couldn't make out a word. I squeezed my eyes shut to protect them.

Paparazzi.

Ian hadn't said anything about the media being here. I supposed it made sense. Rock star parties would provide a lot of fodder for those trashy magazines.

A gentle hand took me by the arm and led me up the steps to the entryway.

"Your name, miss?"

I opened my eyes. A tall, sturdy brunette at my side held a clipboard and an ear piece. She was clearly the gatekeeper and bodyguard to keep out uninvited guests.

"Thanks for saving me. I'm Hope Briars. I should be on the guest list."

"Who extended the invitation?"

I remembered what Ian had told me.

I doubt they'll know who you mean.

Had he been telling the truth? Was the *Damian* image so powerful no one knew who Ian was?

"Ian invited me."

"Who?"

My heart clenched, an ache of sympathy shooting through me.

"I mean, *Damian* invited me."

The bodyguard made a checkmark on her clipboard and stood aside to let me through.

The front door opened onto a vast foyer with marble flooring. Stylish modern furniture had been tucked away in the corners, leaving an empty space in the middle of the room for mingling. Waitstaff with platters of appetizers in their hands maneuvered deftly among the party guests, who barely paid them any attention. It was much more upscale than I'd been expecting.

There were so many people. I didn't recognize a single face. Not personally, at least. A few might have been celebrities I'd seen on TV, but they were different enough in real life I couldn't be sure it wasn't a lookalike.

I was suddenly glad Faith convinced me to wear her dress. Even in this outfit, I felt only moderately fashionable in comparison to the women scattered about the party. I would have been monstrously out of place with my usual leggings.

A wide variety of styles, from classy to glamorous to full on provocative, were on display.

Women in cocktail dresses with subtle gold and silver jewelry held wine glasses by the stems, taking minuscule sips.

A few women with bright red lipstick and voluptuously wavy hair wore pin-up style dresses. Their shapely hour glass figures let them pull off the retro style with ease.

Tall, leggy blondes with plunging necklines and hems barely covering their butt cheeks held audience with handfuls of men vying for their attention.

Despite Faith's best efforts, my dress was too long to be called provocative, my hair and makeup too plain to be called glamorous. But classy? I supposed I could pull it off as well as my sister, if I made an effort.

I wandered further into the mansion, hoping to find someone I recognized. The guests became rowdier and the music louder the deeper inside I went.

Empty glasses and beer cans were strewn about. Couples were making out, half naked, on sofas and against the walls. A group of people were playing a card game, most of them in states of half-undress.

Cameron was there, as was August. Cameron had several bras draped around his neck, with a girl on each knee.

They were deeply involved in their game, so I continued exploring.

The further I got from the entrance, the crazier the party became. Smashed glasses on the floor, trash on every surface, drunk people falling over themselves. So far I'd discovered four parlor rooms, two bathrooms with people passed out on the floor or puking into the toilet, and a handful of what I assumed were bedrooms from the groaning and moaning sounds leaking through the doors.

I still hadn't found Ian. The music was obnoxiously loud. Grimacing, I gave up and made my way back to the front door, surrounding myself with the classy, glamorous women. At least this area of the mansion didn't remind me of a frat party.

I was contemplating leaving when someone bumped into me from behind. I nearly went sprawling across the floor, still not used to the height of my borrowed high heel pumps.

So much for classy.

"Hey, watch yourself." Strong arms caught me before I hit the ground. A familiar spicy scent filled my nose.

Ian.

I wobbled on shaky ankles to right myself. I didn't want to fall and continue making a fool of myself in front of him.

"You gonna be okay with those shoes?" His tone was teasing, but there was a note of concern underneath.

"It's fine." I pretended I wasn't dying of embarrassment. "Someone just bumped into me."

I turned around in his arms. He kept them wrapped around me, gripping my waist with both hands. His hair wasn't styled for the stage. It fell in soft tufts, messy and sexy at the same time. A black band t-shirt clung tight to his chest, muscled arms on display. Silver buckles and zippers adorned his black pants. The rough metal scratched at the skin of my legs, making me acutely aware of how close our thighs were pressed together.

I tried to take a step back, but there was another party-goer directly behind me. Ian pulled me closer before I could get jabbed with an elbow. His body heat sent a flush to my cheeks.

"Damian!" a voice whined. "You said you were going to get us drinks."

I glanced behind him. Two gorgeous women, one on each side, both with fluffy blonde hair surrounding their cherub faces. Each had a pout on her lips, one sour and the other sorrowful.

"Sorry babes." He didn't look at them, keeping his gaze trained on me. "You'll have to get those drinks yourselves."

Both made sounds of disappointment. One tried to reach out to him, but the other pulled her back.

"Let's just go find his brother, instead," one said with a hushed voice. I only made out the words because I was staring at her plump, glossy lips in envy.

Ian didn't seem to hear, his full attention focused on me. Two thumbs rubbed slow circles in the hollow of my hips. My throat closed up as I met his vibrant green eyes. No sunglasses tonight. He was studying me carefully, a sly grin on his face.

"I'm glad you came. You just get here?"

"Yeah. The paparazzi was a surprise."

"Sorry. I should have warned you. The bodyguard give you any trouble?"

"No, but you were right about—" I cut myself off.

He tilted his head. "Right about what?"

"Uh—" I didn't want to tell him about the bodyguard not knowing who Ian was. "You were right, this party is a rager." He didn't notice my slip up.

"These parties aren't always this crazy." He raised his voice to be heard over the din of music and laughter. "But Cam got a little overzealous with invitations and well, you see what happens."

"Do you know everyone here?"

"Most of them."

There had to be hundreds of people at the party, the majority of them women.

Exactly how had he come to know them?

He *was* a rock star, after all. I knew what that meant. If I was going to let Ian flirt with me, if I was going to let him do... other things with me, I had to accept Ian had a past, the same as anyone else. His was simply more colorful than most.

"It's pretty crowded here. C'mon."

Letting go of my hips, Ian draped an arm around my shoulders to guide me through the crowd. I didn't know where he was taking me. I honestly didn't care.

With the touch of his black-lacquered fingertips burning into the bare skin of my collarbone, I would have let him lead me straight into hell.

Chapter 10

As Ian led me through the mansion, I began to get nervous, wondering if maybe he was taking me to a bedroom where we could be alone. Rock stars probably moved fast. Instead, to my relief, he took me to a kitchen. There were fewer people there. A handful of waitstaff were putting together trays of finger food, and a few groups of twos and threes were pouring each other drinks before leaving to rejoin the party. Less than a dozen people. Compared to the rest of the party we were practically alone.

The kitchen was spacious, full of shiny chrome appliances and a marble-topped island table. Just as fancy as the rest of the place.

"Rock stars must make a lot of money." Dammit. I hadn't meant to say that out loud. Ian chuckled, not taking offense.

"Cameron has no concept of moderation. You know he wanted to buy an entire condo building? He wanted each of us to have our own floor."

"Investing in property is smart."

Ian snorted. "Invest? Nah. Cam wanted a place where we could all party together non-stop. Like a frat house. August talked him out of it."

"So he bought a mansion instead?"

"This house is tame. Did you know he was looking at mansions with entire basements turned into indoor swimming pools and helicopter pads on the roof?" He chuckled as my mouth popped open. "C'mon, let's get you a drink."

Ian grabbed a few bottles and a plastic cup. I watched as he put together a concoction, keeping track of the labels, trying to figure out what I would end up with. I didn't recognize most of the brands.

"Here you go." He presented the cup with a flourish.

I took it from his hand and sniffed. "Smells sweet."

"Try it," he urged.

I took a small sip. "It's delicious. It can't taste the alcohol."

"There isn't any."

I paused in the middle of taking another drink, staring at him over the rim. "How young do you think I am?"

"It's got nothing to do with your age."

He stepped closer. I took a few steps back unconsciously. I bumped into the island counter. He didn't stop, just continued crowding me until our bodies pressed together. One of his knees nudged between my legs.

My fingers gripped tightly around the cup, my toes curling inside my high heels.

"Are you worried about corrupting a minor?" Even as I spoke the words, I heard my own shallow breathing, the shakiness in my voice. My breasts touched his chest with every inhalation. "I'm of legal drinking age, you know."

"I don't want you under the influence." He placed both hands on the countertop, one on either side of me. I was trapped. The look he gave me was wicked, hungry. "You're going to remember everything that happens tonight." He leaned forward until our noses were touching. He tilted his head, as if angling for a kiss. "*Everything.*"

My breath hitched. Half an inch closer and—

Ian pulled away. I nearly sagged to the floor. My heartbeat raced madly as I remembered how to breathe.

"You should finish your drink." Ian smirked. "You'll need your energy for later."

I'd been right about rock stars and their smooth moves. I took a long, silent breath to gather myself.

"You think you can feed me a line and I'll fall into bed with you?" I was proud I kept my voice steady. I wasn't going to let him shake me.

Ian threw back his head and laughed. "Apparently not." He took my hand and pressed a kiss to the back. "Does the princess need more wooing from her prince?"

"Prince? I was thinking more of the evil huntsman."

His lips twitched. "You think I'm planning to cut out your heart?"

"Isn't that what you do? Make all the girls fall in love with you then crush their hopes and dreams?"

He gave a casual shrug, but the corner of his lips turned down slightly. "That's more my brother's thing."

"I've heard the rumors, you know." I met his eyes and held them. "They say Damian plays with women the way a cat plays with the mouse. Is that what you're planning on doing with me?"

I expected him to retort with a joke about eating me, but he pulled back.

"Right. *Damian.*" He fidgeted with the leather wrist cuff on left arm. He played with the decorative silver buckles until the nail polish on his right hand came off in chips. "I'm sure you've heard a lot about The Twins."

"I'm sorry." I was beginning to get this was a touchy subject. "I didn't mean—"

"No, it's fine," he interrupted. "I'm just being—" he cut himself off with a wry grin. "Never mind. Let's go back to the party. I'll introduce you to some cool people."

I chided myself for touching on a sore spot, but I wanted to know. Sometimes, with the way he looked at me, I wondered if maybe Ian felt something more than passing lust. But I knew that was exactly what every other girl Ian had gotten into bed probably thought about themselves.

Besides, it didn't matter. If his interest was fleeting, it was all the better. No risk of getting attached.

I allowed Ian to drag me around the party. I thought his *cool people* would be an endless parade of movie stars, musicians, and other celebrities. To my surprise, Ian took me around to meet sound engineers, publicity coordinators, and other behind the scenes people. They all gave him high fives and slaps on the back.

He was genuinely friendly with these people. Maybe I had been wrong. Ian did pay attention to all the little cogs in his entertainment machine. Maybe that's why a lowly intern wasn't too far beneath his notice.

"They all like you," I said as we moved from group to group.

"I'm a likable guy."

"No, but—" I wanted to put it the right way. "I didn't expect you to introduce me to ordinary people. I thought you'd be hanging around your famous friends. You're not..."

"Not a stuck up asshole celebrity?"

"I was going to say, untouchable."

Ian let out a chuckle. "You sure that's the word you want to use around me?" he murmured in my ear.

My heart fluttered again. I hadn't had a steady heartbeat since stepping out of that taxi.

"Yo, Damian, stop monopolizing the fresh meat." Cameron came up from behind and threw his arms around us, sticking his head between ours. He still had three bras hanging around his neck. "Is this asshole annoying you?" he asked me.

"You're the only annoying one around here, Cam." Ian retorted.

"Fuck off." Cameron's grin was still firmly in place. He grabbed my cup and downed the rest of it. "Your girl needs another drink." He gave Ian a pointed stare.

"Is that your subtle way of telling me to get lost?"

"Nothing subtle about it. Get lost."

Ian shook his head, but removed his arm from around my waist. "I'll be right back."

"No, wait—!" My eyes practically begged, *don't leave me alone with him!*

Ian tossed me a wave. "He's gonna get you sooner or later. Might as well be sooner."

I looked on in dismay as Ian retreated.

"*Sooo,*" Cameron drawled out the word, getting in my face. I could smell the alcohol on his breath. "Ms. Image Consultant."

His expression was like a shark scenting blood. He wore his usual dark denim jeans low on his hips and a white t-shirt so tight and thin it was barely there. Thick silver chains hung from Cameron's belt, matching the chains on his wrists. Thick black eyeliner rimmed his eyes. Bright red hair framed his face. He looked like the devil himself.

"Um. Yes?" I tried to hide my nervousness.

"You and Damian fucking?"

My eyes bugged out as I let out a violent series of coughs. He slapped me on the back with enough force to send me toppling over.

"We, we're just—" I stammered once I could breathe.

"Not yet, hmm?" Cameron gave me a smug tilt of his chin. "Too bad Damian called dibs on you. Otherwise..." he tilted my face up with a finger on my chin. "You'd already be flat on your back screaming my name."

"I don't think I would, actually."

"No?" He twisted his fingers in my hair and tugged until our lips were nearly touching. "You sure about that?"

I let out a small whimper.

"Just fucking with you." He laughed, releasing me. "You don't have to worry about me."

"Why? Because *Damian* called dibs?"

"That's part of it."

"What am I, a piece of candy?"

"Nah." Cameron grinned. "As much as I like to flirt, I only fuck groupies, not colleagues."

"Colleague?" I snorted. "I'm an intern."

Cameron patted me on the back again. "Don't sell yourself short."

"I'm an intern," I repeated. "I'm not even getting paid."

"August didn't tell you the important details of the job, did he?"

"Like what?"

"Like your salary."

When Cameron told me, my brain nearly short circuited.

"Oh," I said weakly.

"It's temporary for now, until our album is released. But who knows. If August and Naomi like your work, they might ask you to stay on."

"But why me? There are hundreds of people who would kill for a job like this."

"Not everyone can do what you do."

"I didn't do anything special. I came up with that idea on a coffee break."

"And maybe that's why August hired you. If that's the kind of stuff you come up with on a whim, what kind of stuff can you do when you've got a whole team behind you?"

"No pressure, though, right?" I muttered.

"You kidding?" Cameron shook his head. "*Tons* of pressure. This album is August's baby. You better not fuck it up." He laughed at the terror on my face. "Don't worry. We'll all be there to help you. Damian especially."

Cameron nudged my shoulder. Damon appeared with two plastic cups in his hands.

"Here you go, sweetness."

Damon wore the same jeans and t-shirt as his brother, his hair equally messy-but-hot. His black-tipped nails weren't chipped, but that was the only difference. From this distance, his eyes were strikingly green, no hint of the dark blue I'd seen close up.

"Thanks." I took the cup, wondering where Ian was.

Damon got up close, putting an arm around my waist. I pushed at him and took a few steps closer to Cameron. As if he could protect me. That was as likely as a wolf protecting a flock of sheep.

"Still playing hard to get?" Damon narrowed his eyes at me with a teasing smirk.

He was no doubt trying to make me think he was his brother. Did Damon not know Ian and I had already kissed? I hadn't been playing hard to get at all. Maybe they didn't share everything. Maybe Damon was trying to get into my pants before his brother did.

I took my first sip of the drink to hide my unease when Cameron spoke.

"Your girl and I were having a nice discussion about fucking."

I inhaled my drink down the wrong pipe and sputtered. It was half because of Cameron's words, but half because the drink was strong enough to peel paint. My tastebuds has been seared off. "What *is* this?"

"My own concoction," Damon replied.

I handed him back the cup. "Sorry. I much prefer the drink Ian made me."

90

Both men looked startled. Cameron's eyes darted between me and Damon.

"This is better than the first drink I made you," Damon said, recovering smoothly.

"Ian's drink tasted sweet. This one tastes like jet fuel. Speaking of," I glanced around the room, "where's your better half?"

Cameron was still looking between the two of us, curiosity evident, but Damon's face turned disgruntled.

"He's on his way," Damon muttered, taking a swig from the cup I'd handed back to him without flinching.

Sure enough, within seconds Ian strolled up from behind me. He slung his arm over my shoulder in a casual gesture. The trail of his fingers along my arm and neck was anything but. He pressed a new drink into my hand.

"Have you been properly traumatized?" Ian asked. "Ignore everything Cam tells you. He's a filthy liar."

"Including Damian calling dibs on me?"

Ian stiffened. I hadn't meant to say it out loud. Maybe one sip of jet fuel had been enough to loosen my tongue. Ian seemed to forced himself to relax, but I felt the tension in his arms.

"What can I say? I'm known for being possessive." His kept his tone light and airy.

Damon sidled up to my other side and curled his arm around my waist again. "Of course, I'm much more possessive than my brother. What do you say the two of us somewhere a little less crowded? Get to know each other?"

A brief flash of irritation crossed Ian's face, before it smoothed out. Damon was really getting into it, trying to make me think he was Ian, trying to confuse me. Trying to trip me up.

It wasn't going to work. I knew which one was my Ian.

My Ian.

A jolt of panic went through me.

This was getting dangerous.

I shouldn't be thinking like that. He wasn't *my* anything. He was just flirting with me. He was just having fun.

I swallowed hard.

"Actually," I ducked out from under both their arms. "I think I need to go to the ladies room. Cameron?"

"There are two on every floor," he said, still bemused. "Head down that hall. Second door from the end."

I made my escape before Ian or Damon could protest, sprinting off.

Once in the washroom, I stood in front of the mirror, gripping the sink with both hands.

Was I really going to go through with this?

I wasn't a one night stand sort of person. I was only thinking about making an exception for Ian because, well, it felt like I knew him. I'd been watching him and he'd taken notice of me. We'd talked, we'd kissed.

With Ian, maybe there could be something more.

I groaned and buried my face in my hands.

What was I thinking? He was a rock star. I was an intern. He was flirting with me the way he flirted with all of his groupies. He was interested now but that didn't mean he would stay interested.

I was fine with that. Really. I liked Ian. It felt like we had a connection. But I wasn't going to kid myself into thinking there could ever be anything more. I just needed to get this out of my system.

Besides. I didn't want anything more.

More led to complications. *More* led to heartbreak.

And I'd had enough of that already.

Chapter 11

I finished drying my face with a fluffy white towel and opened the door. Ian and Damon ambushed me the second I stepped out of the ladies room. I flailed, nearly shutting the door in their faces. Ian caught it by the handle and yanked it open.

"No hiding in the washroom."

"I'm not hiding."

The soft, patient look in those green eyes nearly made me melt to the floor.

Goddamn, but I was in deep.

"Why don't we get you another drink?" Ian suggested.

"Not if Damon's making it," I shot back. He wasn't going to ply me with liquor and make me lower my guard.

Ian laughed while Damon looked put out. "I'll make this one, I promise." He turned to Damon. "I think Stacey and Shannon were on the patio looking for us. Why don't you go entertain them?"

Damon gave his brother a probing look. The two stared each other down, communicating without words. After a moment, Damon conceded.

"Sure, I'll go handle Tracey and whoever."

"Stacey and Shannon," Ian repeated.

"Right." Damon gave me one last unreadable look before taking off.

When Damon was out of sight, Ian draped an arm across my shoulder again. He gave me a possessive squeeze as he led me away.

"Just for the record, I want you to know I'm not interested in Damian," I said.

Ian quirked a smile, his chipped nails drawing absentminded circles around my collarbone. "No? Then what are you doing here?"

I dug my heels into the floor, making him stop and look at me. "I'm interested in Ian."

His lips parted slightly in surprise, seemingly at a loss for words. His eyes searched mine.

"In case you thought I want to sleep with your brother," I continued. "Because I don't. I can tell the difference between the two of you. I don't want you thinking I'll take whichever one of you I can get."

There was only one twin I wanted to sleep with.

As if he'd heard my thoughts, Ian's expression changed. The softness in his eyes became heated. The arm around my shoulder pulled me in close, until we were nose to nose, like in the kitchen.

"Cam says you practically choked when he asked if we were fucking."

I fought back a blush. "I just told the truth."

Ian tangled his fingers in my hair, pulling my head back. His eyes glinted with evil humor. "Maybe I should make a liar out of you." He leaned in, angling for a kiss.

I ducked my head, avoiding his lips. "Cameron was asking about The Twins when he made that joke."

Ian growled and tugged until our bodies pressed together. I felt every muscled line of his body through my thin dress. It was getting harder to think, but I needed to make something clear.

"I don't know if there's some weird thing between you and your brother when it comes to girls and sex, but—"

Ian brought his lips crashing down, silencing me with kiss. I whimpered into his mouth, letting his tongue play with mine.

"I'm not letting my brother anywhere near you," he growled into my mouth. "You're *mine*."

A shudder went through me at the possessiveness in his voice.

It was a lie. I knew it was. No girl could ever truly *belong* to him. Ian had his fun and when he was done, he left a trail of broken hearts in his wake.

But I was willing to go along with it, willing to pretend I'd fallen for his lies, as long as he never stopped kissing me.

Ian pressed forward, backing me up until I was against the wall. He didn't let go of my lips once. One hand cradled my head, protecting it. The other touched the small of my back, urging our hips together. I felt the heat of him, already hardening, and let out a small moan into his mouth. Handfuls of drunk party goers passed us in the hallway. None of them paid attention to the rock star making out with a random girl.

The wall behind me disappeared, interrupting a battle of tongues and lips. I yelped, nearly toppling backward. The door we were making out against opened. Ian's arm around my waist kept me from falling on my ass. A giggling couple snickered an apology as they walked out, straightening their clothes and smoothing their hair.

Ian took advantage. He stepped into the now empty room and pulled me in. The door slammed shut behind us. He drew me into the circle of his arms, kissing me desperately.

"Tell me you want this," he whispered against my lips. He held a tight handful of my dress in his fist, the material twisted. I could feel his restraint, could feel him fighting with himself to not tear it off. He pulled back, eyes blazing, hungry and intense. "Tell me you want me."

I heard his unspoken words.

Tell me you want only me.

"I want you, Ian. Only you."

He growled and ravaged my lips, kissing me for long minutes. Our mouths moved together perfectly. He tangled his free hand in my hair, pulling me closer, kissing me deeper.

I pressed my hands against his chest, feeling the taut muscles shifting under his shirt. I clawed into the thin material, tugging at it. He broke our kiss for the one brief second it took to pull it off.

I nearly whimpered at the sight in front of me. Firm, smooth skin, hard as rock. I ran my hands up his chest, my eyes following the path. He was beyond gorgeous.

Ian grew impatient. He lifted the hem of my dress up to my waist. One hand cupped the back of my thigh, bringing my leg up around his hip. The hard length of him pulsed against the thin cotton of my panties.

A flood of heat washed over me. An ache made itself known between my legs. His bare chest hadn't been enough. I wanted to feel it. I wanted to feel him.

I reached down and explored his thick shaft through his pants. Ian let out a soft sound of pleasure, encouraging me to continue. I grasped his belt and slowly unbuckled the strap. He stopped breathing. The sound of the metal zipper drawing down was loud, the only sound in the room aside from our heavy breathing.

Ian hissed as I reached inside and wrapped my fingers around him. The muscles in his shoulders tensed. He was long and thick, burning hot and rapidly hardening under my touch.

I stroked up and down slowly, making sure to use a light touch. He bucked his hips into my hand, trying to get more of that delicious friction.

I pulled back, keeping the pace slow and even. I thought of a thousand different things I could do with that hard shaft. A thousand things he could do to me. My inner muscles clenched and throbbed.

I twisted my wrist as I stroked up the head. Ian's control snapped. He gripped my waist tight and hoisted me up. I wrapped my arms and legs around him instinctively, squeezing with my thighs. Once I was secure he swung us around. He easily lifted me, striding the five steps it took to reach the king-sized bed.

Ian threw me down, watching me bounce a few times from the force of it. I raised myself up on my elbows, taking the moment's reprieve to catch my breath. He kicked off his pants and stood there, looming over me. I wet my lips at the sight of him naked, hard and thick in front of me.

His eyes glinted, mischievous yet scorching hot. "You want me?"

"Yes," I exhaled shakily.

"Take off your dress."

I paused for a moment, meeting his eyes, then pulled it over my head. I was left in my strapless bra and panties.

His eyes blazed as they roved over every inch of me, a predatory look crossing his face. Goosebumps rose up on my arms, shivers running through me.

"Take off your bra."

I complied, reaching behind me to undo the hooks. When it was unfastened, I slowly removed it from my chest, taking my time to reveal every inch of skin.

"Fucking tease," Ian breathed, but the tilt of his lips told me he loved it.

When my breasts were free I threw the bra at him. He caught it out of the air with one hand.

"A souvenir," I said playfully.

"What if I want a different souvenir?" His eyes flashed. "Take off your panties."

My breath caught in my throat. The thin cotton was already damp with desire. I lifted my hips and slid my panties down my thighs, past my ankles. I was completely naked, every part of me on display.

"You want to take these, too?" I twirled my panties around my finger, trying to hide my sudden nervousness.

His wicked smirk made my heart jump. "I'm going to take *everything*."

Mere moments later, Ian was kneeling between my legs. My thighs tried to clamp together automatically.

Ian wouldn't let them. He spread my thighs with both hands, baring me to him. Calloused hands ran up and down my inner thighs. Thumbs rubbed circles on my skin, never quite reaching that one spot I wanted him to touch. The throbbing between my legs turned almost painful. I bit my lip as my inner walls clenched and unclenched. I wasn't sure if I should ask for what I wanted or stay quiet and let him take charge.

He glanced up from my center, eyes meeting mine.

"You want something?"

I swallowed heavily and nodded.

"Tell me," he demanded.

"I want you," I whispered, my breathing uneven. "I want you, Ian."

He darted down and sucked my clit into his mouth. I let out a shriek, my head thumping back onto the mattress, arms no longer able to hold myself up. His tongue flicked and swirled, his lips sucked and caressed.

I let out a continuous series of squeaks and gasps. He played with me as expertly as he played his instrument.

The dark thought that I was just a toy to him briefly crossed my mind. I gave it a brutal shove away. All my attention went to the mouth pulling uncontrollable pleasure from my body.

Ian had me squirming and moaning, my hips bucking underneath him. He was so good at this, *so good*, and I was close to coming apart. All I needed was a little bit more—

Two fingers thrust inside me, curling up and I came with a choked cry. My insides throbbed around his fingers, squeezing them tight. Wetness flooded out of me, coating his hand. Sparks flew across my vision as golden sunshine flowed through me. I couldn't breathe, couldn't think. All I could do was feel.

After long moments, I finally came down from the high. I was sprawled across the bed, trembling, limbs shaking with aftershocks. I craned my neck to find him smirking at me from between my legs.

I pulled him up for a fierce kiss, tasting myself on his lips. Running my hands along his muscled chest, I explored across the vast expanse of his broad, inked back. I wanted to touch him everywhere, to lay claim to every inch of skin.

He allowed me to draw him close, crawling up my body until his cock pressed against my hip. Somehow, he had grown even harder, even larger, while I'd been recovering from my earth shattering orgasm. It felt different. We weren't skin to skin. He must have put on protection while I'd been basking in bliss. I chided myself for not thinking of it sooner.

But I couldn't dwell on it. The feel of that stiff length, burning hot, ignited my lust all over again.

I shifted my thighs until they were on either side of him, tilting my hips up to meet his.

"I want you, Ian," I whispered. "I *need* you."

"How do you want me?" The words were low, teasing. "You want it hard and fast?" He moved his hips in circles, the tip of his cock barely brushing the valley between my legs. I moaned, the throbbing ache inside me rising to a fever pitch.

"Or do you want me to fuck you nice and slow?" he continued. "Want me to draw it out until you can't take it anymore?"

I whined in the back of my throat, squirming and writhing underneath him.

"Hard and fast." I panted, my nails clawing into his back, utterly wanton.

His eyes flashed. "I'm going to make the whole mansion listen to you scream my name."

I squeezed my eyes shut, flushing with both embarrassment and desperate need.

"Tell me," he growled.

"Ian..." I breathed.

"Louder."

I opened my eyes, meeting his, a burning bright green. "I want you, Ian. Only you."

With one swift motion he buried himself inside me. I cried out as his thick cock speared me, inner walls parting around him.

I gasped and panted, trying to take in air through shaky lungs. He stayed still for a moment, letting me get used to his size.

"Shh, sweetheart. Relax." The soft, cooing words were at odds with the hard thrust he'd given me. I throbbed and fluttered around him, that sweet ache inside me only growing stronger.

When my breathing calmed, he pulled out slowly. I exhaled a deep breath. He slammed back in and I cried out again, the desire inside me swelling, spiraling upwards. I clung to his shoulders, nail digging into skin, trying to keep myself from flying apart.

On and on he continued thrusting into me, filling me completely, until he couldn't possibly go any deeper. Then he changed the angle and proved me wrong, entering me even more fully.

I tossed my head back and forth, fingers fisting the bedsheets, trying to contain myself, but it was too late. He snuck one hand between my legs and pressed with his thumb, rubbing in circles. I clenched around him, squeezing tight.

"Ian!" I called out his name as my orgasm came crashing over me in one explosive wave, scorching every single nerve in a fiery blaze.

He let out a soft groan in my ear, his body quaking with his own release. His fingers found mine, lacing them in an almost painful grip.

We shuddered together, breathing heavily into each other's mouths, gazing into each other's eyes as we slowly regained our senses.

Bit by bit our trembling ceased. Ian loosened the painful hold on my hands, but didn't let go. He kept our fingers clasped. I closed my eyes and thumped my head back onto the bed, gasping. I let out a moan as he slipped out of me, feeling every inch of his retreat. Moments later he was back at my side, one hand brushing through my hair. I sighed and relaxed into the mattress.

"I don't think you werc loud cnough."

I cracked open my eyes to find him looming over me, that familiar evil look on his face. "What do you mean?"

"Did you think we were done?" He trailed two fingers down my chest, down my stomach, to the apex of my thighs. I inhaled sharply. "I don't think the entire mansion heard you scream out my name yet."

By the time he was done with me, I couldn't remember my own name, let alone his.

Chapter 12

"What's got you so hot and bothered?"

I jumped, hiding my phone against my chest. Faith leaned over my shoulder for a peek.

Ian had been messaging me constantly since that night of the party, after we'd exchanged cell phone numbers.

"In case I need to get in contact with you for work. Or whatever." His eyes had been full of mischief.

That *or whatever* turned out to be the most explicit dirty talk I'd ever experienced, through text or in person.

I should have known he wouldn't be satisfied with fucking me into exhaustion. He had to continue teasing me about it, too. I wondered when he would give it up.

Or whether I wanted him to.

"Someone sure has a filthy mouth." Faith raised an eyebrow. I hadn't been fast enough to hide the screen.

Despite the late hour she was impeccably dressed, still wearing the slim cocktail dress she'd left the house in. I was sitting on the sofa in the living room with fuzzy pajama bottoms and a tank top, my hair in a messy ponytail. Not for the first time, a pang of envy went through me. She looked as good at midnight as she had when she left for work at six o'clock that morning.

"I didn't write the texts," I muttered.

Her eyes lit up as she removed pieces of jewelry one by one. "You got a boyfriend?"

"No."

"A boy toy?" she amended.

"No!"

"You hook up with someone?"

I ducked my head.

"Tell. Me. Everything." She kicked off her high heeled pumps with a contented groan. "Was it good? Was he hot?" She shook her head as I stammered. "Never mind, I know you're too shy to share the details."

I wasn't shy, exactly. If it had been a regular guy I would have dished everything. But Ian was a rock star. A playboy. He was known for breaking hearts. Faith knew as well as I did what guys were like.

She knew how devastated I'd been the last time I'd fallen for some guy's lies.

If I told her about Ian, she would only worry.

Then again, what Ian and I had was a one time thing. Everyone knew The Twins were the love 'em and leave 'em type. I was in no danger of getting attached, and therefore in no danger of getting hurt.

I couldn't take anymore of that.

But I knew there was no reason to worry. Ian would no doubt move on to the next girl within days.

Although from his text messages, he still enjoyed toying with me.

I re-read Ian's messages as Faith changed into her own pajamas.

So exactly how many times have you touched yourself thinking of that night?

I bet you'll never forget the feeling of my cock sliding inside you.

I loved how ready you were for me. How wet you were.

You made the most delicious sounds when I fucked you.

I should have made you wrap those pretty lips around my cock.

I let out a shaky breath, trying to calm my rapid heartbeat.

Faith came back minutes later. I quickly hid my phone again as she flopped on the sofa next to me. She grabbed for the remote, flipping through channels. I bit my lip, debating.

"If I tell you something, do you promise not to freak out?"

She bolted upright and tucked her legs underneath her. "I knew it! You banged some guy at that party, didn't you?" Her expression turned concerned. "It wasn't one of those rock stars you're working with, was it?"

I knew I shouldn't have told her.

"Hope..." Faith said, worry in her voice. "Are you really sure you want to get involved with a guy like that? You know what that type is like."

"I know exactly what he's like. The kind of guy who can show a girl a wild night."

"And is that the only thing you're looking for?"

"Yes!" I said, exasperated. "It's not like I'm going to fall in love with him. It was a one time thing."

"As long as you know what you're getting into."

I faked a casual expression I didn't quite feel. "He's hot. He's into me. I figured, why not go for it?"

"I guess that's fine. As long as he was a gentleman."

The memory of Ian asking if he should fuck me hard and fast made me squirm. "Um."

"Okay, fine, as long as he wasn't selfish about it."

"He definitely was not."

"That reminds me. I ran into one of those assholes when I dropped off your sketches."

"You saw someone famous? Who?"

"I don't know. Some arrogant jerk. Probably an actor. He came on strong. Like he expected me to fall over myself to be with him then and there."

I snorted. "Sounds about right. Most of the guys I work with are like that."

"Including Mr. Sexting?"

My phone buzzed again before I could answer.

"That him?" Faith asked. "I thought it was a one time thing."

"He just likes to tease me," I mumbled. "He does it to everyone."

As soon as I said it, a lump of something dark and heavy settled into my stomach.

Of course he did it to everyone. He would toy with me for a few days, sending me dirty messages to make me blush, and then he'd get bored and move on.

But they weren't always dirty.

You looked so beautiful lying on that bed, naked and wanting.

Your lips were like heaven.

I loved the way you whispered my name.

I just knew you were something special.

Those messages made me lightheaded and dizzy. They made my heart flutter like a thirteen year old girl with her first crush. They were almost... sweet. Sweet enough to leave me breathless.

But the majority of it was pure and utter filth.

I squirmed, trying to ignore the arousal rising between my legs, trying to ignore the liquid heat threatening to dampen my panties. It was no use.

"I'm going to bed."

"Okay. 'Night." Faith flicked through channels, unaware of my little problem. She liked to unwind with trashy reality TV after a long day.

I headed to my bedroom and closed the door. I slipped under the covers and closed my eyes. I forced myself to inhale and exhale steadily, trying to induce sleep.

It didn't work. I couldn't stop my hand from drifting down my stomach. I couldn't stop myself from going further, until my fingers were between my legs. I was already so wet. I let out a soft moan.

Even with him miles away, Ian still drove me crazy.

Chapter 13

My body buzzed with nerves, both fear and excitement fighting for control. It was finally time to meet with the band to present my ideas for their new concept.

I'd been working on this for weeks, but still stayed up until nearly dawn sketching out last minute ideas before my meeting with the band. I'd only caught a few hours of sleep. I'd proposed an entirely new image and concept for the album on the spot, but I'd barely fleshed out the details myself. I needed something concrete to show them.

How the hell do you represent the rise and fall of a relationship through clothing, photoshoot props, and other material objects? It was one thing to write a song about passionate sex. It was another to have a person embody those emotions physically.

I wasn't entirely satisfied with what I put together, but it was a good start. This was an amazing opportunity. I didn't want to screw it up.

There was one problem, though.

I couldn't suppress the small part of me that quaked inside at the thought of seeing Ian again.

I wondered what he would think of my idea for him and his brother. I also hoped he wouldn't act overtly suggestive in the meeting. I didn't want to get distracted and I knew I wouldn't able to keep my composure if he toyed with me like he'd been doing. Would he be as flirtatious? Or was his attention short-lived? He certainly knew how to throw me off balance. He no doubt thrived on it.

I finished my breakfast then got showered and dressed — a harder task than I anticipated. I didn't know how to dress for the meeting. Should I wear a conservative business suit, complete with white collared shirt and blazer? I wanted them to take me seriously as a professional. Then again, they hired me for a creative job. Should I accentuate my individuality and be avant-garde? Show them how much of a fashion forward person I was?

I couldn't stop a small thought from bubbling to the surface. I wanted to impress Ian. I wanted to be sexy. I wanted to be irresistible.

I wanted him to be as affected by me as I was by him.

Unfortunately, none of those styles were really me. Faith was right — I didn't have much in my closet aside from sweater dresses, leggings, and oversized shirts. I shouldn't have left the decision of what to wear for the morning of.

I decided to borrow from Faith and mimic my boss. Janet was chic but professional. A black pencil skirt, ending right at the knee, along with a bright red peplum top. It hugged my every curve in just the right way. The outfit paired well with a skinny black belt and matching high heeled red pumps, to accentuate my legs. I wasn't comfortable in heels, but damn if they didn't make my legs look hot.

I could imagine Ian's eyes skimming along my body's silhouette. The thought made my insides throb.

My usual messenger bag got switched out for a black leather purse with metal spikes along the seams. I wanted more of a rock and roll style than usual. Armed with a portfolio case filled with sketches I'd hastily drawn up the night before, I was ready to go.

When I arrived at work, I stopped a few feet down the hall from the conference room. I straightened my shoulders and made myself walk into the meeting with a confidence I didn't quite feel. Fake it 'til you make it. That would be my motto.

The moment I stepped into the room, all my confidence shattered.

Not only was the entire band there, not only was my boss Janet there, but the Director of Product Development *and* the band's manager Naomi were there.

Every eye swung to me.

"Hope. How nice of you to join us." Janet's voice was snide.

I quickly glanced up at the clock on the wall. I was two minutes early. My heart still thumped wildly. I was frozen under those stares. The stares of people who were so much more important than me. I tried to force a pleasant expression onto my face, but barely managed to make my lips twitch upwards.

My savior swooped in to rescue me.

"Well, look at you, sweetheart. You're dressed to kill."

Ian pushed back from the conference desk with a kick of his heels, the leather chair wheeling back. I gripped my purse tight, still frozen, making my eyes focus on Ian and not dart around the room nervously.

He approached me with an easy stride. "I wouldn't expect anything less from our new Image Consultant." He plucked my portfolio out of my hands. I reached out reflexively, trying to grab it from him, but he held it out of reach. He flipped through the pages and whistled out loud.

"Fine Arts degree, huh? Maybe my Picasso joke wasn't so far off. Take a look, guys." Ian tossed my portfolio on the table, sketches fluttering everywhere.

"Be careful with those!" I admonished without thinking. "They're the originals, not photocopies."

"Protective of your work?"

"You ruin one of my sketches and I'll dress you in a paper bag." I bit my tongue the moment the words left my mouth.

115

Ian laughed and guided me to a chair with a hand on my back. That light touch sent sparks up my spine. The heat of his hand was like an iron-hot brand on my skin, even through my blouse. When we reached an empty chair, his hand left my back, fingers trailing along my hip, indecently close to my ass.

I willed myself not to blush and sat gingerly, smoothing my skirt. Even behind his sunglasses, I could feel Ian's eyes burning into me. Exactly the response I'd hope for.

I surveyed the table. It was disconcerting being on the receiving end of so many stares. It should have been the Director, my boss's boss, who intimidated me. Instead, it was the members of Darkest Days who made my chest clench.

I nodded politely to the table, unsure where to begin.

Once again, Ian came to my rescue.

"Janet, Hope used to work for you. Why don't you introduce us?" he suggested.

Janet's mouth pinched, annoyed at being ordered around. I jumped in.

"I believe I already know everyone." I turned to the woman sitting at the far end of the table. "Kristine Watts, Director of Product Development?"

Of course I knew who she was. She was my boss's boss. I interned in her department. She'd been one of the people interviewing me for the position. Her dark blue eyes glinted behind her glasses. They didn't hold a hint of recognition, not that I expected it. She didn't have time to memorize the names and faces of all the interns.

"And Naomi Sera, Darkest Days' manager."

Naomi gave me a no-nonsense nod, not unfriendly, but brisk and business-like. Her dark hair, cut short in a bob, was almost severe. She must have chosen that cut on purpose, to make up for her baby face. I knew she was at least in her thirties, but didn't look much older than me.

With those introductions out of the way, I moved on to the band.

"Of course, I know the members of Darkest Days already. Noah Hart, Cameron Thorne, August Summers, Ian and Damon Drake."

Damon narrowed his eyes at me. I swallowed hard and looked away.

"And this is Hope," Janet said. "She's an intern with Product Development."

"Not anymore."

All eyes turned to August. He faced me, but it was like he was staring right through me, a look of concentration on his face.

"Now that we've all been introduced," Naomi said, "Tell us about the concept you thought up for our promotional photo shoot and first music video."

This was what I'd been nervous about. I didn't know if they would like my preliminary ideas. *I* didn't know if I liked my preliminary ideas. I'd barely had time to think them through.

I took a deep breath and dove in.

"To start off, we need to talk about the stages of a relationship and how to represent them. When it comes to the clothing, we can't be over the top. It's got to be subtle. They still need to have a cool rock star style. Here are my basic ideas." I spread out the sheets of paper where I'd jotted down some ideas and quick line sketches. "First is the courtship stage, right?"

Everyone nodded, waiting for me to continue.

"You put your best foot forward, act on your best behavior. You're the gentleman. You're the romantic. At least at first. You need to hide your flaws. Your inner demons. You don't want to scare them off too soon. You need to ease them into it. Reveal your dark side slowly. Cameron." I nodded at Darkest Days' bassist. "That's you."

Cameron wore a tight grey t-shirt. It shouldn't have been surprising — this was a business meeting after all — but I rarely saw Cameron without his abs on display. The lack of chiseled muscle transformed him. His sexy bad boy image was softened, his face cute and earnest. He was less like a sex god and more like a member of a boy band. Maybe that was why he often went shirtless.

Cameron leaned back in his chair with a pleased expression. "Are you saying I'm secretly a demon?"

"In the sack, apparently." I hadn't meant to say that, but Cameron just laughed with a smug tilt of his chin. I was glad he hadn't called me out on the gentleman part. There was something about him off-stage. Something less wild. Something softer.

I was positive Cameron would hate being called soft.

"For Cameron's concept we're going with a sort of Jekyll and Hyde theme. I'll see if I can come up with something not too cliché."

"I like it," Cameron said. "Can I have clawed nails and glow in the dark eye contacts for the Hyde side?"

"Sure. Why not."

"Sweet."

I turned to Ian and Damon. They wore jeans with matching band t-shirts, black with a silver graphic. Their hair stuck up in soft tufts, not coiffed into spikes like they preferred during concerts, but untamed, disheveled.

Unlike Cameron, whose off-stage persona had softened into something like boyish charm, The Twins looked even more devastating. No one should be that damn sexy so early in the morning. Or maybe it was the heated smirk on Ian's lips making me feel that way.

Breathe, I told myself.

"The next stage is the conflict stage. Passionate fighting, followed by passionate make up sex. That's you two." I tried not to blush at the lascivious quirk of their lips. "Damon is the fighting. He'll be wearing ripped clothing, torn and bloodied. Ian is the—" I paused to make sure my voice didn't waver. "—the sex. He'll be wearing something less harsh, something romantic but sexy. Like silk and leather."

I would never dare tell a soul, but half the reason I came up with the idea was because I wanted to see Ian dressed up in silk and leather.

"It's a cool idea, but it won't work." Damon was brisk, dismissive. "We don't want a different image. We want the same look for the both of us."

"I just thought—"

"No." His word was final.

I deflated. I'd been so sure I was on the right track. I'd have to re-think my entire idea.

I snuck a glance at Ian, expecting him to be as adamant. His lips were pressed in a thin line. Anyone else would have thought he was annoyed at the idea of two separate looks as well, like his brother.

But I didn't think that was it.

Maybe Ian liked the idea of two separate images. Maybe he didn't want to be the exact same as his brother. That would have been surprising. Everyone treated Damon and Ian like they were practically the same person.

Was Ian getting tired of it?

"What comes after the conflict stage?" Naomi asked.

I brought my thoughts back around to the present. I could dwell on Ian and his psyche later.

"Next is the break up. August, you'll be the one to represent that. You're in pain all the time. It's like you're drowning. You're choking on tears. You don't know how you're going to live with the pain, but you don't know how to show it. You don't know how to ask for help. You feel lost and alone."

August's eyes went from distant to focused within an instant, giving me a piercing stare.

He was the most professional of the bunch with a white collared dress shirt to go along with black skinny jeans. He was well respected in the industry, not only for his talent with practically every instrument known to man, but also for his genius composing. He also acted as producer for both his band and others.

He wasn't just a rock star. August was a prodigy.

This prodigy also happened to be giving me a shrewd look. I hoped he wasn't reconsidering his decision already. I tried not to be intimidated by it and continued.

"There's some cool fabric so shiny it looks wet. I'd like to make your outfit using something like that. I'd also like to have underwater shots for the music video."

"Literally drowning in tears," August murmured.

"That's the idea."

"And Noah?" he asked.

The scowl on Noah's face was nothing I hadn't seen before. I didn't take offense. It wasn't directed at me. He wore his usual spike-studded leather jacket even though it was warm inside the building. The jacket and scowl combined to give off a vibe that visibly said "fuck off."

Noah's dark eyes flickered to me before going back to stare at the wall. Cameron shifted in his seat, leaning back and putting his hands behind his head in a casual pose. His leg jerked under the table.

Noah flinched, letting out a faint grunt. The lead singer gave Cameron such a dirty look I thought the bassist would be set aflame on the spot.

Cameron threw him a shit-eating grin, and nodded his head towards me, silently telling him to pay attention.

"Noah's the last stage of the relationship. His heart was walled off. He was covered in spikes. But some of his walls are starting to come down. Some of those spikes are falling off. He's starting the healing process. He'll slowly learn to love again."

Noah let out a strangled noise.

"You did say she was perceptive," Damon muttered to Ian under his breath.

Maybe I'd touched a nerve.

"I like it." Kristine gave me an approving nod. I wriggled a little in my seat, happy the person in charge of all Product Development praised my ideas.

"It's not bad." Janet said grudgingly. Maybe she hated being one-upped by an intern. At least she wasn't shooting me down.

"We can run with that," Naomi agreed. "We'll need much more detail, though."

"This was a basic outline of my ideas," I said. "We can continue working on them together."

"So what about us?" Ian said.

"We want a new look," Damon continued.

"Give me a few days," I told them. "I'll come up with something you'll both like."

Damon wanted to be the same.

Ian wanted to be different.

I wondered how the hell I could pull that off.

Chapter 14

That had been my last meeting for the day. Even though I wasn't needed at the office, I was going to have to go home and continue working. The Twins needed a different concept. Something similar but different. My heart sank the longer I thought about it. I had no idea what I was going to do.

I rode the elevator to the first floor, took one step out into the street and smacked face first into a muscled chest.

"Sorry!" I apologized quickly, bending to pick up my fallen bag. "I wasn't watching where I was going."

"I was."

I stood up and found myself face to face with Ian.

"I was watching you very closely." He slid a hand down my back to grab a handful of cheek, squeezing gently. "Your ass looks fantastic in that skirt."

I swatted his hand away and backed up, holding my purse in front of me like a shield. "I wasn't thinking of my ass when I chose it."

Despite pushing him away, I wanted his hands back on me, caressing every inch of my skin, sliding lower until his fingers were between my legs.

My breath caught in my throat as I stared into those green eyes. Eyes I hadn't been able to stop thinking about.

"You heading somewhere?"

"Just back home. I've got to start re-working that concept."

Ian's face turned dark, clouding over with frustration.

I had to ask him. "Did you like my idea?"

The expression on his face smoothed out as he gave me a deceptively casual shrug. "It wasn't a bad idea, but Damon and I both want the same concept."

"Do you?"

Ian pierced me with his stare. "Yeah. We do."

I knew Ian understood I'd meant the singular *you,* but he'd answered for both of them. I decided to let it go for now.

"I pretty much spent the entire week holed up in my room getting ready for my meeting with you guys. I don't know how I'm going to come up with another concept in only a few days."

"You're smart. I'm sure you'll think of something."

"I don't feel smart. I feel lost."

"The others all liked theirs. Three out of four isn't bad."

"I don't know if Noah liked his."

"Noah can go suck a dick. He doesn't like anything." He tilted his head at me. "You need a ride home?"

All breath left my lungs. Alone in a car with Ian. I didn't think my heart could take it. "No. I'm fine."

"Where are you parked? I'll walk you to your car."

"I don't have a car. I've got a public transit pass."

Ian blanched in disgust. "Now I'm definitely driving you home." He stepped towards the curb and nodded towards the car parked directly in front of the Etude entrance. "Get in."

The car was shiny and black and sleek. "That's yours?"

"It's my baby," he said with something almost like pride.

"I don't think that's actually a parking spot."

"Says who?"

I pointed to the *no parking* sign three feet away.

Ian squinted at it. "Is that new?"

"Pretty sure it's been there for years."

Ian hummed, then turned away, ignoring the sign. "You coming?" He held the passenger door open, waiting expectantly.

"Really, I'm fine. You don't need to drive me home."

"I don't *need* to. I want to."

"Ian—"

"I'm not leaving until you get in. You wouldn't want me to get a ticket, would you?"

"As if you couldn't just pay for it with the change in your pocket."

"Still waiting." He looked at his wrist as if he were checking a watch.

"Women always give you what you want, don't they?"

"Yes." The smug tilt of his lips and glinting green eyes should have annoyed me. The heated expectation I saw in his expression made me dizzy instead.

I gave up and slid inside.

The interior was pristine, all black leather and sparkling clean. Even though I didn't know anything about cars I knew this one had to be expensive. I didn't want to touch anything for fear of leaving smudged fingerprints. I kept my feet tucked together and my hands in my lap.

Ian got in on the driver's side and peeled away from the curb with a squeal. "You ever been in a Hennessey Venom GT Spyder before?" he asked.

I clung onto the seat, afraid for my life. "I assume that's a type of expensive car?"

Ian laughed. "So that's a no. You're not a car person?"

"No. I'm not an obnoxiously rich person, either."

"Does it bother you?"

"That you guys get paid a billion dollars while we interns work for free? Gee, of course not. I'm perfectly happy with that level of income disparity. I love living off ramen noodles."

Ian gave me a small smile. "Sorry. Should have known what the answer would be."

"It's weird. Living vicariously through you guys, with all your fancy cars and enormous mansions and raging parties. It's almost like I'm a rock star myself. I'm not used to it."

"I'm still not used to it either. I—" Ian glanced at me. "I didn't have this kind of money growing up."

"No normal person has your kind of money."

His mouth downturned at the corner. "Point taken."

I felt bad for mouthing off when he was clearly trying to share something with me.

"So you've played guitar for a long time?" I asked, bringing us back around to a less sensitive subject.

His eyes lit up. "Damon and I bought used guitars from this garage sale when we were twelve. We practiced every day until we finally sounded halfway decent. Started this stupid garage band with our friends when we were thirteen. We never looked back."

"You got any demos from that band I can listen to?" I joked.

"Yeah, but we were shit," he laughed. "We recorded ourselves through the crappy speakers on our computers. It was awful. We felt so proud though."

"You should feel proud. Starting a band as a teenager, recording songs, that's impressive."

"We mostly just fooled around. We only played together for two years. But it was a hell of a lot of fun. The music helped distract us from the shit show that was—" he stopped abruptly, with a snort. "Nevermind. Let's not even get into that."

I waited for a moment but he didn't continue.

"How did the music help you?" I asked softly.

He was silent for a moment, as if contemplating what to say. "I don't want to be a downer," he murmured at last.

My interest was piqued. "My life hasn't exactly been a joyride, either. I—" I bit my lip before continuing on. "I want to know more about you."

He flicked his eyes to me briefly before turning back to the road. "Damon and I always knew we wanted to pursue music. Our parents didn't agree. We... left home."

I heard the slight pause in his voice. "Left home, or were forced to leave home?"

He quirked a sad smile. "Always so perceptive." He tapped his fingers on the steering wheel in a nervous pattern. "Our home life wasn't the greatest. Our dad had a temper. Sometimes—" he cut himself off, face going blank. He gripped the steering wheel tight, the leather squeaking. After several silent, awkward moments, he relaxed his grip and gave an easy shrug. "Anyway. We were better on our own."

"How old were you?"

"Fifteen."

"Did you have someplace to go?"

"We crashed on friends' sofas sometimes. We busked for money. We made do."

"That's how August found you, isn't it?"

Ian frowned at me. "What? How did you know that?"

"You told me before that August found you playing in a shitty garage band. But you said you only played together for two years. You couldn't have been in a band while you were homeless. You lied."

His lips quirked. "Yeah. I lied. Sorry. I didn't want to get into my whole sob story. Anyway," he shrugged, "the truth is close enough. Damon and I were jamming together on a street corner. August was walking by, on his way to check out some proper bands, scoping out some guitarists. It was like fate."

"It must have been wild, going from *that,*" I gestured to the street outside the window, "to *this.*" I gestured to the interior of his luxury car.

"Wild doesn't begin to describe it."

"Homeless at fifteen. No wonder you're not used to any of this rock star stuff."

"You have to agree, though, I've adjusted to the lifestyle quickly." He flashed me a forced grin.

I sensed the change in our conversation's tone. Perhaps Ian had shared as much as he was going to.

"It's awesome your hobby became your career."

"What about you?" He nodded his head to the file folder full of sketches in my lap. "You always been obsessed with art and stuff?"

"My parents got me this little kid's art kit one year for Christmas. Cheap watercolors, colored pencils, stencil notebooks, things like that. I didn't think much of it at first. It sat on my bedroom shelf for a good six months. One day I got bored and pulled it out. The moment I put pencil to paper I knew I'd found something special. Of course," I added, "I wasn't any good in the beginning, either. And no, you're not allowed to see any of my childhood artwork."

"So you've always been an artist," he mused. "How'd you come to work at Etude?"

"I just applied for an internship like everyone else. I suppose because of my artistic background they decided to put me in the Product Development department."

A look of consternation appeared on Ian's face. I help my hand up to stall his protests.

"And I know musicians hate to be called *products*, but that's essentially how you guys are viewed by music execs."

A crease appeared between his brows for a brief moment, but soon smoothed out. "So you were already helping artists develop their image?"

"Well. Not technically. My job was to do whatever my boss told me, whether that was ironing outfits, picking up clothing from the dry cleaners, or making sure each band member had the right accessories before performing."

"I can testify you did well with that last part."

"Glad to hear I did something right."

"Are you worried you're not doing a good job? You shouldn't doubt yourself. You scored this internship for a reason. They must have seen something in you."

"I no longer feel completely out of my depth, at least."

He frowned. "Why would you feel that way?"

"Are you kidding? My first day as an intern was nerve-wracking. I'd shown up at this tall office tower in the heart of downtown. The height of the building is nausea-inducing. That avant-garde exterior design, all angles and glass? It's something out of a futuristic sci-fi film. I'd known Etude Entertainment was one of the top entertainment companies in the world with all its rock bands, actors, and other celebrities, but it hadn't sunk in until I saw the building housing your headquarters. I was *this close* to just turning around and walking away."

"I hadn't thought of it that way. I'd probably be intimidated, too."

"I can't imagine anything throwing you off guard. You seem pretty..."

He lowered his sunglasses, pulling them over his eyes, and gave me a cocky grin. "Confident?"

"I was going to say full of yourself."

He laughed. "I have a feeling spending time with you is going to cure me of that."

Spending time with me. Surely he just meant professionally. For work. He couldn't mean anything more personal.

"But you obviously didn't walk away that first day. What made you decide to stay?

"I snapped a quick picture and texted my sister. I just said *intimidating, much?* She wrote back, *get your ass in there.* She knew me enough to know what I was thinking."

"Anyone would be overwhelmed to be working with rock stars."

I let out a snort. "Until a few days ago, I'd barely had any contact with people who weren't just interns and assistants like me. You know what I did for my first week? Organized a closet."

"Seriously?"

"Seriously. On my first day, I was shown to a room full of studded belts, thick soled black shoes, lengths of chains, and other accessories. None of it organized, most of it on the floor. My very first task was to make sense of it all."

"How glamorous."

"Maybe not, but I wanted to do a good job anyway. I put myself to work and within days the room was spotless. Every item hung up or placed in a drawer, all color coordinated by season and style. Ever since then I've been the one responsible for artist's accessories."

"Is there really that much work for something like that?"

"Not all the time. For something like a small concert at a club, you guys wear whatever you feel like, right? But larger events needed more coordination. The marketing team would throw a fit if the clothing you wore in an interview or during a photoshoot didn't fit the image the department was trying to sell. Sometimes it feels like everything is staged. Nothing is authentic. As a music fan, it was disheartening to find out."

Ian frowned. "We have a say in our image, you know. No one's going to force Darkest Days to dress, or act, or speak, in any way other than what we felt like."

"I get that. It's just the Marketing and Product Development's job to make sure *whatever the band feels like* is consistent."

"And that's why we agreed to hire you, I suppose." Ian's lips tilted into a smirk. "Well. That's why August decided to hire you. I had an entirely different motive altogether." The car squealed to a stop in front of my apartment. "Looks like your chariot has delivered you to your castle, sweetness."

"Still trying to play the part of the prince?"

"Nah." He flipped his shades up to reveal his eyes, that brilliant green staring me down. "Playing the evil huntsman who catches the princess is much more fun."

The carnal grin on his face made me flush as I fled his car, slamming the door closed behind me.

Why did he get off on teasing me so much?

I turned back at the last minute. Ian was still out front, watching me. Making sure I got inside safely.

Was this all just a game to him?

Or was it something more?

Chapter 15

A few days after Ian had driven me home and we'd gotten to know each other better, I planned on attending another Darkest Days concert.

Once again, Janet almost ruined my plans with another last minute task. I wanted to tell her no. She wasn't my boss anymore. But it wasn't technically true. I still worked in the Product Development department.

"Please, Faith!"

I had to plead with her again. Janet wanted me to drop off a box of accessories. I was supposed to bring it to the office the next morning, but of course Janet wanted it immediately. If I did, I'd be late for the concert.

"This is the second time," Faith grumbled.

"I know, but *please?*"

"Ugh. Fine."

I threw my arms around my sister. "You're the best."

"That's twice you owe me."

"I promise I will pay you back. Somehow."

"She's not your boss anymore."

"She's sort of my boss. I guess. I don't want her to be upset with me."

"You need to learn to stand up for yourself, Hope. You can't let people keep walking all over you."

"I'm an intern. It's my job to let people walk all over me."

But was it? I was Darkest Days' Image Consultant now. Did Janet have any say over whether or not they kept me on after the album was done? I wanted to stay on her good side just in case. Or, at least, I didn't want to be any more on her bad side than I already was.

Thanks to Faith, I made it to the concert in time to see Ian before he went on. The bouncer let me inside when I showed him my staff badge. The place was swarming with people getting ready, assistants and sound techs and all the other cogs in the machine helping Darkest Days' career move smoothly.

I was off work, technically, although anything having to do with Darkest Days could serve as an inspiration. Seeing them in concert again would give me more ideas, especially watching at this distance. I was as close as I had been at that concert where Ian first noticed to me.

Ian and the guys were probably in the artists lounge, getting hyped up for the show. I wondered if I should head over, but thought better of it. They'd probably want alone time to get ready. Besides, I didn't know if I was ready to see Ian yet — especially not in front of all his band members.

Another group was playing on stage. I recognized the frontman, with his golden hair, curls flopping over his forehead, and smooth, seductive voice. Kell, the excessively vain yet somehow still charming lead singer of Feral Silence, Darkest Days' rival band.

Feral Silence was the group who stole August's concept. Well, stole was a harsh word. I had no doubt they came up with the concept on their own. Still, it galled they had gotten to it first, forcing us to rethink our strategy.

On the other hand, if they hadn't, I wouldn't have my current job. Maybe I owed them thanks.

Feral Silence's set was amazing. Kell didn't disappoint, his voice ranging from low growling to high pitched screaming, and hitting every note in between. Jayce, the guitarist, wore no shirt under his leather jacket, no doubt to show off his impressive abs and smooth dark skin. The speed of the song had his fingers flying over the fretboard in a near blur. Their bassist, Ren, had long black hair falling over his shoulders. The glossy strands tossed back and forth as his body surged with the beat. Morris pounded furiously on the drums, keeping the band in perfect time, despite the theatrical way he played with his sticks.

They were nearly as good as Darkest Days. I knew I was biased, though. I was sure fans of Feral Silence would say they were better than any other band who performed that night. But I still thought Darkest Days was the best.

When Feral Silence finished their final song, they threw picks, water bottles, and drumsticks to the crowd. Any and everything that wasn't nailed down was sent soaring. After several long rounds of cheering and begging for an encore, they thanked the audience and left the stage, leaving disappointed moans in their wake.

Anticipation buzzed through me. Darkest Days was up next. I'd been a fan for years. Getting to know the band personally hadn't dampened my enthusiasm for their music in the slightest. I glanced around to see if the guys were ready to go on.

My heart nearly stopped. Ian was only a few feet away, dressed for the stage.

There was just something about rock stars that turned girls into mush. Ian was no exception. I'd watched him in concert many times, but that was before I'd seen him naked. Now, every single piece of clothing only served to enhance the gorgeous body I knew lay underneath.

Tight leather pants accentuated the hard muscles of his thighs. They were slung low on his hips, revealing the tantalizing V-shape of his lower abs, leading to...

I lifted my eyes before I could be caught staring.

It didn't help any. The moment I saw the thin t-shirt stretched tight around his taut chest and muscled upper arms, I was done for.

I finally looked up to meet his eyes, the barest hint of kohl making them a brilliant green, with a smirk holding a dozen filthy promises.

My stomach clenched. My panties were getting damp from the sight, my insides aching. I'd never been able to control my physical reaction to him.

"Hey there, Ms. Fancy Consultant." Cameron drew my attention away from Ian by throwing an arm around my neck and tugging me close. "Better put that tongue back in your mouth before you start drooling."

I snapped my mouth shut.

Cameron's eyes were dark and smokey, his usual on-stage style, with shimmering bright red hair. "You keep on staring at *Damian* like that and I'm going to get jealous."

"You don't sleep with colleagues."

"I could make an exception." He grinned in my face.

"Get your hands off my girl." Ian strode over with a grim face, pulling me into his side.

Cameron raised an eyebrow. "She's your girl, now? That's cool, man." He pecked a kiss on my cheek. "You two kids enjoy yourselves tonight."

"Is he really jealous?" I asked as Cameron sauntered off, bass guitar in hand.

"He knows you're not interested. Pissing me off is his way of having fun."

The light smudge of black rimming his eyes was doing something to my insides. Guys shouldn't be hotter in eyeliner than girls. It wasn't fair. Ian caught me staring. He ran one finger along my neck, black nail polish smooth and gleaming.

"I like that look on you."

"What look?"

"Like you want to eat me alive."

I flushed. I couldn't exactly deny it.

I'd told myself to forget about it and move on. I'd gotten laid. It was out of my system. One guy shouldn't still have so much power over me.

My body disagreed.

"Can we do it again?" I blurted. I wanted to bury my face in my hands, my cheeks burning with embarrassment. But I couldn't take it back. All that sexting, all that teasing, all that leather and eyeliner, had done me in. I had no more willpower left.

"Do what again?"

Ian's eyes glinted with mischief. He knew exactly what I meant, but he was going to make me say it. I steeled myself, speaking the words in one long breath.

"I know better than to expect any sort of commitment from you and you rarely sleep with the same girl twice but I don't want us to be a one night stand." I held my breath for his response, expecting annoyance or exasperation.

Instead, Ian gave me a wicked grin. "I know, right? That night at the party was fucking awesome. I definitely need more of your magical puss—"

"Stop!" I clapped a hand over his mouth.

"I'm just saying." The words were muffled against my palm. "The sex was too good for it to be a one time thing."

I lowered my hand. "So you're saying you want to do it again?"

"And again and again and again." Ian snickered at my blush.

"So what is this, then?" I asked. I wasn't naive. I knew I could never expect a real relationship with Ian, no matter how mind-blowing the sex was. That wasn't how it worked with The Twins.

He glanced away from me for a moment, as if he were thinking. Then he flicked his eyes up to mine. "Friends with benefits?"

"That implies you'll be sleeping with other people at the same time and—" I squirmed, "—I'm not sure I'm comfortable with that."

Ian tilted his head, considering me. "What about a fling?"

"A fling?"

"Yeah. We have sex a couple more times, get it out of our systems. We have our fun like mature adults, then go our separate ways. Call it a brief love affair."

My heart nearly jumped out of my chest at his use of the L word. Again.

"You can make all your friends jealous." Ian's eyes sparkled, like he was getting excited on my behalf. "A short, whirlwind romance with a rock star."

I knew better than to ask for anything long term, but I didn't want this to be over. Not yet. "A fling, you said?"

"Nothing wrong with a fling, right?"

"Showtime, guys," August called. He flipped one drumstick between his fingers in an impressive repetitive motion, heading over to the stage. He was usually the first one ready to go, as the others were usually, as he put it, *fucking around.*

In Damon's case, sometimes literally.

Ian pressed his lips to my ear. "Now, as much as I'd love to have those pretty lips on my cock, I've got a show to do, sweetness."

Arousal flooded my entire system. I wanted to drag him into the nearest storage closet and do exactly that — wrap my mouth around his thick length and consume him whole.

He moved from my throat, trailing fingers along my collarbone to the swell of my breasts. "Maybe I should wear leather and eyeliner all the time, if it gets you this worked up."

I squirmed, unable to look away from those burning eyes.

"Now you know how I feel when you walk around in those sexy little skirts of yours."

Ian's lips curved up at the corners. His eyes narrowed into a seductive gaze. That was when I knew. I knew I was in trouble.

This man had the power to break my heart, and I was practically ripping open my chest and offering it to him.

I was so going to regret this.

But I didn't have it in me to resist.

Chapter 16

"Shattered glass."

"What?"

"Shattered glass," I repeated.

Ian and Damon had the same look of confusion on their faces. I fumbled with my sketches, switching the papers around to face them, so they could see what I meant.

"There's a type of material that appears to be shattered glass. It's pliable, so it can be used in clothing. Damon, you're the fighting. You're throwing things around. You're in a fury. You're breaking things. Your material will be dark, like obsidian, but it will glint in the spotlight. Ian, yours will be reflective. Like mirrors. The sex was so passionate. You slammed her up against the door. You broke the mirror on the wall. The mirrored glass will reflect everything, expose everything, because you're exposed to each other. Your hearts are raw and wide open."

I'd stood from my chair, both palms pressed flat on the table, arched forward to get in their faces. I leaned back, easing up on some of the intensity.

"There are tons of ways we can do this in videos and photoshoots, but the most important part is your physical appearance. I've got that figured out. I'm thinking of making you each a vest with the material. You can wear it over your normal clothing and take them off to switch places. And I know you love your wrist cuffs, so we can make new ones matching the vests."

The Twins stared at me, not speaking. Their eyes weren't hidden behind shades. Instead, the sunglasses were perched on top of their heads. The expressions on their face were identical, but unreadable. I tried not to wilt under those dual gazes.

"I mean, it's just an idea. We don't have to go with that."

"It's cool," Damon said after a moment.

"I love it," Ian added.

My heart lifted. "Awesome!" I hated that my voice sounded so squeaky. I lowered my tone. "That's great. I'm glad you like it." It had only taken me days to come up with the idea. "I'll start sourcing the material right away."

"How did you decide which one of us was which?" Ian asked.

"Does Damon seem like the angry, fighting type?" Damon continued. "Or do you like to imagine Ian having sex?" His eyes glimmered with amusement.

A flush threatened to consume my entire body. "I wasn't thinking about the sex, necessarily." I tried to quickly figure out how to explain my reasoning. "When I think about the two of you, Damon seems more brash. More likely to argue about things. More stubborn."

Damon narrowed his eyes at me. I swallowed hard, but continued.

"Ian, you're more... seductive, I guess. You're passionate, but in a different way. You'd grab onto your girl and kiss the breath out of her to stop the arguing."

Ian's eyes widened in surprise. He opened his mouth to speak.

"And how are you so sure it's Damon who's always arguing?" Damon asked. "It could be Ian you see acting like a pain in the ass all the time."

"Maybe you're both a pain in the ass." Ugh. I'd let my mouth run off again. "I just meant, there are some differences between the two of you. It made sense to style you each in those ways."

As hard as they tried to be identical on stage and in interviews, I noticed the differences between the two. Even though everyone else struggled with it, it wasn't difficult for me to tell them apart. It was even more obvious ever since I started working at Etude and had the opportunity to watch The Twins in person.

Okay, I had to admit it. I hadn't been watching The Twins.

I'd been watching Ian.

147

The surprise on his face has faded into something else. With narrowed eyes and a wolfish grin, Ian wasn't the energetic, carefree rock star who teased his fans like they were mere toys to play with. Instead, his eyes were intense, resolute.

"Whatever. I'm glad it's taken care of." Damon stood abruptly. "I was worried we were going to look stupid or boring."

"Nothing boring about this," Ian murmured. He was practically undressing me with his eyes. My breath hitched. I couldn't look away.

He turned his attention to his brother and I was released from his spell. I took a shaky breath in.

"I'll take care of everything right away," I said after several false starts, brandishing my sketches. The ache between my thighs told a different story. I needed to go take care of something entirely different.

"See ya, sweetheart." Damon strolled out of the room. Leaving me alone with Ian.

That wolfish grin spread wider. Ian stood and stalked around the table until he was mere feet away.

"So you think I'm seductive?" he drawled.

I froze in place, pinned by the weight of those words, by the hidden promise beneath them. He ran his eyes up and down my entire body. I could feel his lips on my skin. My thighs clenched, warmth flowing from my pink cheeks to my core. When he was within inches of me, he stopped and tilted his head.

"I asked you a question, sweetness." He pulled me towards his chest with an arm around my waist. I stared into his eyes, frozen. He lowered his head until his lips just barely touched mine.

We were too public. Anyone could walk in and see us.

I couldn't make myself care. My terror wasn't strong enough to overpower the effect Ian's mouth and hands had on me. One touch was all it took for me to surrender. A wave of heat ran through me, flooding my every nerve, centering between my legs.

"I don't have any more meetings for the rest of the day. Maybe we could take a break and..." I left the rest unsaid.

His eyes flashed with heat. "At work?" he teased. "Naughty girl. Aren't you scared of getting caught?"

"I could perhaps be persuaded."

"Looks like I managed to snag a girl with an exhibitionist streak."

Ian closed the office door and locked it. Pushed me up against the wall. Pressed his hips into mine.

"So tell me..." His eyes glinted in the dark. "Exactly how dirty do you want to get?"

All sorts of naughty thoughts ran through my mind, but there was one in particular stood out.

I pushed myself closer and felt him against my hip. I tiptoed my fingers down his chest, his sides, until I reached the zipper of his jeans. He hissed when I pressed my palm against his length. I unbuckled his belt, pulled the zipper and gently palmed his rapidly stiffening cock. He let out a strangled grunt.

I caressed the shaft gently at first, with short, small strokes. His already large girth was expanding with every second. I rubbed my thumb over the tip. He buried a groan in my neck. As his breathing got heavier, I stroked faster, twisting my wrist and thumbing the head.

He bucked into my hand, trying to take control. I pulled back slightly, slowing the pace again, only giving him the barest of touches.

He growled in my ear and grabbed both my wrists, pinning them behind my back. My eyes grew wide with surprise.

"You like teasing?" His voice was low in his chest.

"Not as much as you do."

He chuckled darkly. "So you enjoyed all my messages?"

"I don't know if enjoyed is the word I would use."

Reading his words to help bring myself to orgasm multiple times was bit more intense than just *enjoyed*.

"Which one was your favorite?" he whispered in my ear. There was a wicked curve to his lips.

"I—"

"Was it when I said I loved how wet you were?"

I inhaled sharply.

"Was it when I said loved the sounds you made?"

My breath hitched.

"Or maybe when I said I want those pretty lips wrapped around my cock?"

I whimpered. He let out a pleased hum, knowing he'd got me. He knew how much I wanted him. How much I wanted to taste him, to feel him on my tongue.

He tugged on my hair, tipping my head back until our eyes locked. That brilliant green, full of need and want, nearly took my breath away.

I wanted more of that needy look. I wanted him to fall apart completely. I slowly lowered myself to my knees. I kept my eyes trained on him, reveling in his burning hunger.

His cock bobbed in front of my lips, drawing my attention. I rocked back on my heels, taking stock of that thick length. Hard, weeping, standing straight out from his body. It twitched with every flex of his abs, as if seeking the wet warmth of my mouth.

I placed one hand on his thigh to keep myself balanced. With a careful touch, I wrapped my other hand around him, pumping once, slowly.

He let out a soft sound from the back of his throat.

My tongue darted out, a quick lick, tasting him for the first time.

He grunted and tightened his grip on my hair. From the trembling of his hands, I knew he was trying not to push me onto his cock. I leaned up and pressed my pursed lips against the head. His whole body went tense.

I parted my lips and took him in one slow, wet slide. Ian let out a long moan, his whole body shuddering.

I paused there, more than half his cock fully in my mouth, listening to his strained panting. His thighs trembled under my touch. He swallowed heavily and took a deep, calming breath in.

On his exhale, I slowly pulled back, using a tight suction, dragging my tongue along his cock the whole way. He let out a groan and fisted my hair tighter.

"Sweetheart, you're killing me."

A sweet sense of satisfaction pulsed through me. It started in my chest, squeezing my heart, then made its way to my core. I clenched my thighs together as wetness gathered between my legs. This was turning me on as much as it was him.

If he was hard before, he was rock solid now. I stopped teasing and began a steady rhythm. I let him slide in and out of my mouth and across my tongue. I didn't go too deep, taking him slightly more than halfway.

With every withdrawal I sucked on the head and swirled with my tongue. Ian couldn't help bucking his hips slightly, wanting that heated suction.

I teased, bobbing down a few inches, then pulling back, swirling and kissing and licking. He growled and cupped my face with both hands, one on my cheek, the other stroking the underside of my jaw. I could feel his restraint, could feel how close he was to thrusting in.

I finally gave him what he wanted. With one quick movement, I sucked his cock down until the tip hit the back of my throat.

"Fuck!" Ian slammed a hand against the wall, stopping himself from toppling forward.

I forced my throat muscles to relax. Like before, I waited until he had his breathing under control, then slid my lips back to the tip. He let out a continuous series of gasps and grunts as I bobbed up and down, back and forth, taking him all the way, then retreating.

I knew he was close when he tugged on my hair frantically. "Hope, I can't—"

I gripped his thighs with both hands, keeping his hips still, keeping him in my mouth. I sucked harder, using my lips and my tongue to take him over that edge.

With one choked cry, he fell forward, fists clenched in my hair. The warm, slick taste of him coated my tongue in spurts. I kept my mouth clamped and swallowed, wanting to take everything he had to give me.

After several long moments, the flood subsided. He let out one long shuddering moan. I leaned back and let him fall from my lips. I licked every last drop along the way.

"S-stop," he groaned. "Too much."

I pressed my forehead against his abdomen. The muscles shifted with every heavy rise and fall of his chest. My lips curved into a smile as the grip on my hair eased up and fingers softly sifted through the stands. He pressed a kiss to the top of my head and curled his arms around my shoulders, bending forward to envelope me. I basked in his embrace.

Eventually he relaxed and let me go. I stood up on aching knees and tucked him back into his pants.

"Fuck, sweetheart, that mouth of yours..." he tugged me to his chest and plastered his lips to mine. "I've never felt anything like it," he murmured.

A pang of hurt shot through my chest. Those were the last words I wanted to hear after what we'd done. I pulled back. "Don't compare me to other girls."

His brow furrowed, distressed. "I'm sorry. I didn't mean to."

"I'm not going to be like the others. You can't make me fall for you with pretty words."

I wasn't going to let that happen again.

"That's not—" He closed his eyes, frustrated. "I swear to you, that's not what I'm doing."

"Really? So you don't say that to all the girls?"

"Hope, I swear to you, you're not just another notch on my bedpost."

"Then what am I?" This conversation was getting too serious, too close to a topic I didn't want to examine. But I had to know.

"You're—" he stopped, tilting his head and giving me a piercing stare. "I don't know what you are."

"Gee, thanks."

"No, I mean it." He shook his head, hair falling into his eyes. I resisted the urge to push it back. "I don't know what this is. But there's a connection between us." He cupped my face, bringing my head up to meet his eyes. "From the moment you called out my name after that concert, I knew you were..." he trailed off, glancing away. "This sounds so fucking stupid."

"What? I'm what?"

Those green-gold eyes flicked to mine. "You're different from the others."

I let out a sharp bark of laughter without meaning to. "Seriously? You're going to use that line on me?"

He groaned and leaned forward to rest his forehead against my shoulder. "I know! I told you it's stupid."

"You don't have to sweet talk me to get me into bed. It's too late for that."

"It's not sweet talk. It's the truth."

If it was only a line, if it was only something he said to all the girls, I didn't care.

I wanted him.

I watched him grumble as he struggled to buckle his belt. Sexy, gorgeous, and all mine.

I focused on smoothing out my own rumpled dress. I had to remind myself. He was only mine for now. This wasn't permanent.

But despite the voice in my head yelling a multitude of warnings at me, I was dangerously close to falling for a playboy rock star.

Chapter 17

After that afternoon in the office with Ian, I threw myself into my work. I needed a distraction to keep from obsessing over him, and his possible feelings for me, and my growing feelings for him.

With the guys getting ready to wrap up recording, there was plenty to do. I worked long hours with the Marketing and Product Development departments. I was put in charge of overseeing clothing fittings, working with tailors and seamstresses to make sure each outfit fit perfectly. The guys had to look their best.

That's when my plan to avoid obsessing over Ian completely failed.

I was stuck in a room with half naked rock stars, including the smoking hot guitarist I'd been sleeping with. And I had to be the one telling them to take off their pants. I didn't think my heart could take it.

The guys were professional about it — mostly. Cameron couldn't keep himself from cracking a few naughty innuendoes.

"Couldn't wait to get me naked, could you?" He unbuckled his belt and unzipped his fly, not taking his eyes off me once. "You don't have to pretend it's for work. I'm more than happy to strip for you any time you want."

A few well-placed elbows in his ribs made him eventually shut up. It didn't stop the shit-eating grin from taking over his face.

When Cameron stripped off his t-shirt to try on his outfit, I didn't blink. I'd seen his naked chest enough times it had no effect on me.

We'd worked hard on Cameron's outfit. It was split in half, like Two-Face from the Batman comics. The right side had one pristine white suit pant leg and a matching half-cape. He was shirtless underneath, as per his request. The left side, for his "demon" persona, consisted solely of one tight black leather pant leg. It was the accessories that made it. Clawed, bloody nails, a glow in the dark eye contact, and one bat wing sprouting from his shoulder blade.

I'd worried the half-and-half style would end up being ridiculous, but Cameron pulled it off with ease. He especially loved playing with his half-cape. He draped it around the interns and pulled off courtly ballroom moves, dipping them for pretend kisses. Surprisingly, he played the part of the chivalrous prince quite well.

August's outfit consisted of a tight white top and black leather pants so shiny and slick they looked like liquid ink. One could almost think he'd jumped into a pool and came out soaking wet, which had been my intention.

I left Noah's fittings to one of the older, more brusque assistants.

I was still a little wary of him. We hadn't spoken much at all, and he always appeared to be in a bad mood.

His outfit wasn't too far from his usual. For him, we'd put together a black leather jacket, half-adorned with spark spikes, their tips dripping with fake blood. We all had to move carefully around him, so we didn't accidentally get poked.

When Noah took off his shirt, my jaw nearly dropped. My eyes swept up and down his chest, drinking in the sight without meaning to. His abs were something most guys could only dream of, a rival to Cameron's.

Someone cleared their throat. "See something you like?"

I jumped. Ian stood behind me, his lips twitching. I didn't know whether he was trying not to laugh, or trying not to frown.

I ducked my head, embarrassed I had been caught staring. "I didn't know Noah was so, ah—" I tried to think of another word for drool-worthy, "—built. He's always wearing that leather jacket."

"You got a thing for hot lead singers?" Ian's tone was light, but there was a biting tone underneath his words. Maybe he was jealous of Noah.

The thought that he cared enough to be jealous made my heart flutter.

I wanted to reassure him, but we were in the middle of work, surrounded by other employees. I couldn't very well tell him he was the only one I wanted to see naked.

Ian must have sensed my internal conflict. He gave me a devastating look and cupped my cheek. "No worries, sweetness." He spoke the words out loud in a teasing tone. "I know I'm the only man for you." He ran a finger down the side of my neck, making my insides melt. I suppressed a whimper.

The few assistants and interns who were paying attention to us shook their heads and rolled their eyes. They were used to his antics.

That melting feeling solidified into a lump in my throat. Of course no one thought anything of his flirting. Ian and Damon did it to all the girls.

I took a step back, jerking away. Ian dropped his hand, surprised.

"I see you haven't undressed yet." I tried to keep my voice steady, professional. "We should get you outfitted."

Ian did frown then, tilting his head and examining me closely. I forced a smile on my face, pretending everything was fine. "Let's get started."

I should have left Ian's fitting to someone else, but I knew I wouldn't be able to resist staring at his half naked body. At least if I was the one doing the fittings, I'd have an excuse to stare. And touch.

The fitting went smoothly as Ian tried on the various clothes we'd made for him. He would need multiple outfits to last him the entire promotion cycle.

He was particularly enthusiastic about his and Damon's matching vests.

"This is fucking *awesome*." He'd put it on over his shirt and looked this way and that in the mirror, getting every angle. "It's like I'm literally covered in shattered glass." He smoothed his hand over the material. "It's not sharp, though."

"It's not real glass," I reminded him. "The fabric was just designed to appear that way."

Ian poked at one of the shards, stabbing with his finger.

"Quit it!" I swatted his hand away. "I've only been able to find enough material for one vest so far. I don't want you poking a hole through it."

Instead of replying, Ian took off the vest and threw it over my head, covering my face. I grumbled and tried to fix my messed up hair.

"If you're mean to me, I won't give you the best part."

"What's the best part?"

I reached into one of the boxes of accessories. "Matching wrist cuffs."

I knew The Twins had some sort of obsession with those things. I'd never seen Ian or Damon without a pair on both arms. I'd used the last bits of material to make the cuffs, using a base of thick black leather.

Ian's eyes lit up as he made a grabby motion. "*Awesome.* Gimme."

I held the cuff out of range. "I don't know, you've been pretty bad today, what with all the teasing. Do you think you deserve a reward?"

Ian threw me lascivious smirk. "Sweetness, you've got no idea how bad I can be."

My breath caught, both at the words and at the tone in which he'd said them. "Fine, then." I tried not to sound breathless. "Give me your old one. We'll try on this new one to see if it fits." I held out my hand, waiting.

I was taken aback when his whole body stiffened. Ian's eye darted around, as if he were nervous. I had no idea why that might be. I tried to lighten the mood, dangling the bracelet in front of his nose.

"Don't you want to try it on?"

He visibly forced his shoulders to relax. "I'm sure it fits, sweetheart. I'll try it on later."

I paused, looking at him with considering eyes. Why did he not want to take off his wrist cuff? He had reacted the same way at the party.

I'd seen Ian with gauze under the cuff one time during their practice session. He said he'd hurt himself on the hand dryer.

Was the wound still sore? Maybe there was a scar. Maybe he didn't want me to see something marring his otherwise perfect body.

I knew rock stars could be vain, but I hadn't thought Ian was like that. It was cute.

I decided to let the subject go. "It's fine, you can try it on whenever."

The tension around his eyes eased up. "So what else you got for me? Special rock star underwear?"

"You can wear your own underwear under your outfit."

"Maybe I won't wear any at all." He winked.

Which of course only made me think of his cock. I fought back a flush and shot back. "Then it's your own fault if your skin gets rubbed raw."

"That just gives you a reason to kiss it better."

I was never going to win at this game. Ian held all the cards, all the chips, practically the entire casino at this point. He kept me so off balance, and he knew it. He reveled in it. He was toying with me, just like all the rumors said he did.

The worst part was, I loved it.

When the fittings were done, the rest of the band had to leave and go back to the recording studio. I stayed behind to clean up, leaving me privy to intern gossip.

"They're so talented," one of them, a red head, sighed. Her hair was the same bright red as Cameron's. Probably not a coincidence.

"I still can't believe I got this internship," a blonde girl gushed. "I've loved Darkest Days since the very beginning. I'm so lucky I get to work with them."

"Yeah, there weren't many internship spots to go around, were there?" I asked.

Four girls gave me piercing looks. I blinked. The stares weren't hostile, exactly. More... calculating.

"Word is, you got promoted to some sort of position high up," Red Hair asked.

"I'm just an intern," I insisted, though I still wasn't sure that term applied to me or not.

"You're working with the Directors of Marketing and Product Development," the blonde said. "Janet has been bitching about you for weeks."

"Oh god. What's she saying?"

Red Hair answered. "Just grumbling about upstart interns and no-talent hacks."

I felt oddly hurt. Janet clearly didn't see the same things in me August had. Maybe I wasn't all that special.

"But from what I've heard, the band loooves you." She drawled out the word and rolled her eyes. "Especially Damian."

I fought back a blush. "I haven't been working with them much. Mostly trying to stay out of their way. They probably don't care enough about me to have an opinion." Better to not make these girls jealous.

"Whatever," Red Hair shrugged. "It's encouraging to see there's a chance for something bigger after these internships, you know? If one of us can make it, maybe the rest of us can."

The girls nodded their heads in agreement. They weren't upset at all. I breathed a silent sigh of relief. The last thing I needed was jealous colleagues. I already had to deal with Janet talking about me behind my back. I hoped nothing she said got back to August. I didn't want him rethinking his decision.

"So dish." The third girl's blue eyes were shining and eager. "Give us all the details."

"About what?"

"Everything! What are the guys really like? Are any of them seeing anyone seriously? Do you know if they ever date interns?"

Red Hair swatted her friend. "Date? You think any of them pay attention to one girl long enough to call it dating?"

Blue Eyes pursed her lips. "You're right. There's always rumors about the guys dating models and actresses and stuff, but never fans."

Blondie snorted. "Yeah, groupies probably get the one night stand treatment."

"Hero worship probably gets old after a while," the fourth, who'd been quiet up until now, spoke up with a soft voice.

"Maybe the trick is to pretend we hate them." Blondie faked a grimace. "I'm *so* not a fan of Darkest Days. Their music sucks. Feral Silence is a much better band."

Red Hair clapped a hand over Blondie's mouth. "Don't joke like that. You'll jinx us or something."

"Guys like girls who play hard to get." Her words were muffled behind the palm.

That didn't explain me and Ian. I'd practically let him molest me from the start.

"Don't suppose you could put a good word in with Cameron for me?" Blue Eyes asked. She had been the one to ask about dating.

"You sure?" I asked. "Cameron is definitely not the dating type."

"I'd take one night with Cameron over nothing." She gave a wistful sigh. "A delicious memory to last me a lifetime."

My chest squeezed tight. That's exactly what I was doing, wasn't it? Spending as much time with Ian as I could before he kicked me to the curb.

"You've just got a thing for his hair," Red Hair accused her friend.

"So says the girl who dyed her hair the same color as his."

The girls all laughed.

My phone buzzed. The girls were chatting to each other, not paying attention to me. I snuck a glance at the screen.

Cam's having another party tonight. You wanna go?

I thought of what the girls said about playing hard to get.

I dunno, I've had a long day. Maybe I'll just stay in and relax tonight.

He didn't reply for several long moments. I panicked.

Maybe I shouldn't have said it.

Maybe he didn't like doing the chasing.

Would he set me aside as soon as he thought I was too much work?

My phone finally buzzed again. I almost dropped it in my hurry to check it.

I promise I'll make it worth your while.

My heart pounded with relief. I quickly texted him back. I was never going to try playing games with Ian ever again.

If you put it that way, I suppose I could make an appearance.

After all, Ian was supposed to be the one playing with me.

Chapter 18

Cameron's latest party was a lot less rowdy this time around. No trash on the floor, no broken glass, no people making out in corners or puking in bathrooms. Ian told me Cameron had kept the invitations to a minimum.

"Only about a hundred people this time," he reassured me.

Only. I didn't think I knew one hundred people. I certainly didn't know one hundred people well enough to invite them to a house party.

In fact, I could probably count on two hands the number of people I would feel comfortable partying with.

But here I was, surrounded by strangers. Celebrities and rock stars and groupies. The only people I knew were the members of Darkest Days. I was at least on friendly terms with Ian and Cameron, even if I hadn't gotten to know August and Noah outside of work.

As for Damon, well, the less he saw of me, the better.

The moment we stepped through the door, Cameron appeared beside me with a handful of bras strung around his neck.

"C'mon, losers. We're finishing up another round of cards." His bright red hair was wild and untamed as usual. "You should join in on the next hand."

He shoved us toward a small crowd of people sitting around a dining room table with drinks in their hands. Most were in states of half-undress.

"Are you playing strip poker?" I asked nervously. "I don't think—"

"Nah," Cameron waved aside my concerns. "We don't play poker anymore."

"Anymore?"

"It stopped being fun after a while. Noah always won and August always lost pretty much ninety percent of the time."

"Noah doesn't seem like the type to have a good poker face."

"He doesn't," Ian said. "He just always looks pissed off so we can never tell when he has a bad hand."

"And August?"

Cameron snorted. "For such a genius, that man is shit with numbers."

"Idiot savant." Ian smirked.

"It's like he has no concept of strategy. He'll have the *worst* hand and keep on betting and raising the stakes until he loses everything." Cameron shook his head in mock sadness. "Pretty pathetic."

"If it's not strip poker, why are all these people half naked?"

"We don't play strip *poker*," Ian stressed.

"So what do you play?"

Cameron let out an evil cackle. "You ever heard of Go Fish?"

I stared at him in disbelief. "That's a game for six year olds."

"Perfect for Cameron." Ian gave the bassist a friendly shove.

Cameron pretended to throw a punch at him. "Don't get cocky, asshole. Everyone knows how much you suck at this game. You're always the one left bare assed naked."

"It's impossible to be bad at Go Fish," I said, still unbelieving. A group of rock stars playing a children's game. "It's literally a game of chance. There's no strategy involved."

"Then I guess he just has shit luck," Cameron declared, elbowing Ian in the ribs.

We reached the table as the group set up another round. August glanced up briefly from shuffling the cards. "You guys want in?"

"I'm not sure—"

Cameron cut me off again, pushing me into a chair with a firm shove. "Hells yeah they want in."

No one listened to my protests. August dealt me a hand. I slumped in my chair, eyeing Ian. He took a seat beside me, pleased and smug. Was he planning to get us both naked? I was fine with that, in theory, but not in front of a room of people.

"It's not fair." There were six people around the table. Ian, Cameron, August, me, and two pretty brunette girls. "The girls are at a disadvantage. We wear a lot less clothing. Panties and a dress, maybe a bra, and that's it."

"Jewelry and accessories count," one of the girls reassured me. She had an oval face and perfectly plucked eyebrows, giving her a classical look. The kind of look I wished I could pull off. "With the amount of bling we wear, sometimes it's the guys who get taken for a ride."

"So how's it work?"

"You know how to play Go Fish, right?" August's usual distant expression was gone. He shuffled and dealt the cards with a laser focus.

"Sure. You ask the person on your left if they have a certain numbered card. If they do, they have to give it to you. If not, they say Go Fish and you pick up a card from the deck. The goal is to play as many numbered pairs as you can until your hand is empty."

"Pretty much."

"But where does the stripping come in?"

Cameron grinned. "Every time you have to pick up a card, you lose a piece of clothing and put it in the middle of the table."

"We don't make it too easy, though," Ian explained. "Whenever you play a pair, you can take a piece of clothing back from of the pile."

"And no one says it has to be your clothing, either." From the bras hanging around Cameron's neck, I inferred that was his main strategy.

"And do those poor girls ever get their clothes back?"

"Only if we ask nicely." The other girl blew a kiss in Cameron's direction with a grin before turning to me. "Hi. I'm Jen. I'm dating Noah."

"*Dating* Noah?"

I couldn't imagine Noah getting close enough to anyone to actually date them. A one night stand, maybe. But a real relationship?

Jen laughed. "Not exactly the most open or affectionate of men, I know. Still, once you get to know him, he's just a big softy underneath."

Cameron snorted. "His Royal Highness is about as a soft as a brick."

I suppressed a giggle at the nickname. It suited him. The lead singer of Darkest Days did sometimes act like a stuck up prince looking down on his subjects from a lofty throne.

"You just need to learn how to handle him," Jen said. She nodded her head towards the other girl. "And this is Natalie. She's dating Morris from Feral Silence."

My mouth popped open, speechless. An embarrassing squeak left my throat. I flushed bright red.

"Hope's a huge fangirl," Ian explained.

"Don't worry, so was I," Natalie reassured me. "You should have seen the way I freaked when I was first introduced to the guys." She gave me a curious look. "Are you..." she paused for a moment, before continuing smoothly, "...friends with Ian?"

My heart thumped so loudly in my chest, it was a wonder everyone couldn't hear it. "I'm working with the band as an image consultant."

Now it was Natalie's turn to gape. "Oh my god, that's so cool. I wish I could work with rock stars."

"It has its moments. Mostly it's just stressful."

"Dealing with this lot is always stressful," August murmured.

The game went about as well as I could have hoped. We went around the table a handful of times, each of us losing and picking up articles of clothing as our turns came and went. I wasn't doing too badly. I lost a bracelet and both shoes at first, but I'd picked the shoes back up again with two pairs in a row.

August's turn came again. His ice blue eyes barely blinked, flicking from one card to another as if they held the secrets of the universe.

"Do you have..." He paused for a long moment, staring intently at Natalie sitting to his left. She inched away from him, nervous. The silence lingered, all of us holding our breath as if something of great importance was about to happen. "...a five?"

"Go fish." She flopped back in her chair, relieved the tension has broken.

August unbuttoned his shirt and tossed it into the pile. I let out a small noise in the back of my throat, but quickly cut it off. August was still wearing a thin white undershirt. His toned upper arms were the kind that made girls squeal. He took a card from the deck and slid it carefully into his hand. He hunched over his cards, eyes narrowing in thought, blond hair falling over his face.

"You got a two?" Natalie took her turn, asking Jen to her left, who handed a card over silently. She played a pair and took a shirt from the pile, pulling it over her head.

Jen looked at Cameron. "Do you have a six?"

He chuckled darkly. "Go. Fucking. Fish."

"Ugh. Fine." She took off her sparkly blue sequined tank top and picked up a card, leaving her in a strapless bra.

"Better stop losing or your boyfriend's gonna be upset you're flashing everyone," Cameron said.

"Better stop taking all my clothes or my boyfriend's going to clock you one in the mouth," she said with a sweet smile.

"Wait," I said. "There's a rumor the girl who helped Noah write his song started dating him. Was that you?"

Jen's smile went soft, almost sappy. "Sure was."

From her glowing face, it looked like she really was in love. She must have been something, to be able to work with, and snag, a man like Noah Hart.

"I heard an early leaked version your song," I told her. "It was awesome. I loved it."

"Thanks!"

"Speaking of His Royal Highness, why isn't he here?" Ian glanced around the room. "Shouldn't he be sullenly glaring at any man who ogles Jen's half-naked body?"

"He and Morris went off to get drinks," Natalie explained.

"And they're not afraid to leave you two alone with Cameron?" I asked.

Cameron winced and placed a dramatic hand over his chest. "Fucking ow. Has my reputation gone that far south?"

"Despite what you might have heard, Cam does have *some* standards," Ian added.

"I know I come off like a lecherous fiend, but I'd never touch another man's girl. Not once he's made his claim." Cameron took a swig of his beer and turned to Ian. "Got a queen?"

"You're cheating," Ian accused as he handed it over.

It was the fourth time in a row Cameron had guessed correctly. He was going to win at this point. Cameron took Jen's blue top from the pile of clothing.

Jen arched an eyebrow. "You better hope I win that back before Noah gets here with the drinks."

Cameron's eyes sparkled. "What would be the fun in that? I love seeing High Royal Highness with his feathers all ruffled."

August reached out for his beer, not lifting his eyes from his cards. He nearly knocked it over. I shot out my hand to keep it from tipping. He didn't notice, making uncoordinated grabby motions in the air. I placed the bottle in his hand. He wrapped his fingers around it without a second glance at me. How much had he had to drink so far?

"You got a jack?" Ian asked, nudging me to get my attention.

Ian was already shirtless. I had avoided looking at him, not wanting the others to see me drooling. He'd also lost his shoes, his pants, and was now down to his boxers. If I didn't have a jack...

I quickly scanned my cards. I had to suppress the upward twitch of my lips, not wanting to laugh at Ian's misfortune. "Nope. Go Fish."

He bitched and grumbled, but stood up to take off his boxers. A flash of silver on his wrist got my attention.

"Hey, just take off your wrist cuff," I said.

Ian froze, going stiff.

"So you don't have to strip completely," I explained.

"It's fine." He seemed to force a smile on his face, but the muscles in his shoulders and back were still tense. His fingers were twitching, trembling. "I'm cool with losing the boxers."

"Jewelry counts, though, right?"

He let out a strangled sound and shook his head.

"That's not fair to you. The rest of us can use our accessories."

"I said it's fine!" He snapped his jaw shut and turned his head away. I shrank back into my chair alarmed. The table went silent.

"I fold," he muttered after a few awkward moments. He threw his cards on the table, grabbed his pants and stalked off down the hallway.

"You can't fold, asshole!" Cameron called out. "It's Go Fish, not poker."

"What was that about?" Jen asked.

I shook my head helplessly, hurt and confused. "I don't know why he got so upset."

"You should go after him." August glanced up from his cards for a brief second, his eyes clear and penetrating. "Don't let him be alone."

I looked back to the hallway. "I fold, too."

"That's not how it works!" Cameron griped as I stood from the table and left.

Chapter 19

I entered one of Cameron's many bathrooms with hesitant steps. Ian was leaning against the sink, taking a long swig of beer. With his head thrown back, his rippling throat muscles and strong jaw were on display. He'd put his pants back on, but he was still shirtless. The sight made my stomach clench.

"Ian?"

He ignored me, finishing off the beer and tossing the bottle in the sink. The glass made a clattering noise, loud in the empty bathroom. A lump of worry formed in my gut. I didn't know what I'd said to make him run off.

"I'm sorry."

He braced himself against the counter with two hands, head bowed. I could see the top of his head in the mirror above the sink.

"No." He exhaled heavily through his nose. "I'm sorry."

"I said something to upset you."

"It wasn't you. I shouldn't have—" He cut himself off and shook his head. "Never mind."

I approached him slowly. I wrapped my arms around chest from behind.

"Can you tell me what I said that upset you?"

"It doesn't matter."

He had his hang ups about his brother, about *Damian's* reputation with women, and now this.

"I don't like feeling I have to walk on eggshells around you," I confessed quietly.

He groaned and turned around, pulling me against his chest. "I don't want you to feel that way."

A vice squeezed my heart. The way he looked at me, the way he held me... was it possible he did feel something for me?

"I wish you'd tell me."

He buried his face in my hair. "I can't."

My heart sunk. "Okay. I get it. It's personal." I shouldn't have gotten my hopes up. I was just a fling to him. There was no reason why he would confide in me.

He shook his head. "It's just, I've never talked about it with anyone."

Whatever *it* was. "Even with Damon?"

"Damon knows. We don't bring it up."

I went quiet for a moment, thinking. "I'm worried."

"About what?"

About you, I wanted to say. *About us.*

But there was no us. Not officially.

"I'm worried I'll say the wrong thing and you'll get upset again."

"I promise I'm not upset with you. I'm dealing with my own shit." He ducked his head, until we were face to face, his hair tickling my forehead. "Okay?" His bright green eyes glittered with sincerity.

"Okay."

I was about to suggest we return to the game when hands slid down my waist. He grabbed two cheekfuls of ass and squeezed.

"So why'd you come chasing after me?" he asked, a playful note in his voice. He rubbed and caressed with magic fingers, causing a warm tingling sensation between my legs.

"I wanted to make sure you were okay." My breathing was already becoming heavy.

"Are you sure you didn't want to get me alone in an empty bathroom?"

"If I wanted to get you alone, I would have cornered you someplace classier."

"Who said anything about being classy?" He trailed his lips along my neck, leaving brief, sucking kisses. "Sometimes it's more fun to get dirty."

A fresh flood of heat coursed through my body. Between his lips and his fingers, my panties were at risk of becoming damp.

"We can't—" I stuttered, torn between pulling away and pushing closer.

Ian cupped a hand between my thighs. My legs nearly fell out from under me. "We can't what?" He rubbed his finger back and forth slowly, teasing.

"We—"

He slipped a finger inside the elastic of my panties and pushed inside me. The rough slide of it made me instantly wet. I let out such a pathetic, needy noise I was almost embarrassed for myself.

"You were saying?" He nibbled on my ear, tracing it with his tongue.

I clenched hard, throbbing around him. My hips rocked forward against my will, wanting more of that delicious friction. I moaned and Ian let out a quiet hum of pleasure.

"That's it, sweetheart. Let go."

He was doing this to distract me. To keep me from prying, from asking more questions. But when he slipped a second finger inside me to join the first, I couldn't bring myself to care. I clutched at his shoulders, keeping myself upright.

He slid his fingers in and out, slowly at first, then increasing the pace to match my racing heartbeat, my soft, hitching breaths. With his other hand, he lowered the straps of my dress and bra off my shoulders. His lips followed the path, leaving a trail of kisses.

He maneuvered my arms until the straps were loose and dangling. A quick snap of his fingers and my bra came undone at the back. One sharp tug on the hem of my dress and my front was bare to him, my breasts on full display. He spun me around, pressing me against the sink, my back to his front.

"Open your eyes."

My eyes kept fluttering closed with pleasure. I fought to obey his command. Through partially opened lids, I saw a reflection of my own flushed face, mouth open and wanton. I saw my own bare chest, dress pulled to my waist, nipples hard and cherry red.

I ducked my head, embarrassed to see myself like that. "I really wish we weren't in a bathroom."

"What difference does it make?"

"Because then I'd feel less trashy doing this."

Ian tweaked one nipple with a sharp pinch. I gasped, head shooting up.

"I want you to watch, sweetheart."

With my eyes fully open, I was met with a stunning sight. Ian's hand on my breast, one black-tipped nail lazily circling a nipple. Ian's deft fingers, plunging into me with long strokes, shining and slick.

Our eyes locked through the mirror. It was too much, too intimate. I gasped his name. His eyes were blazing hot, nearly scorching me with their need.

"I'm going to make you come, Hope." He murmured in my ear. "You're going to come on my fingers while I fuck you with them."

I whimpered at the words, an orgasm tingling at the edge of my senses. I pressed my ass up against his front, feeling his thick length. The small moan that escaped my lips only made him chuckle darkly.

I spread my legs wider apart and tilted my hips. He took the invitation and slid a third finger inside, stretching me, filling me, bringing me that much closer to my release. I bit my lip to keep from crying out.

"Don't do that." He nipped lightly on the curve of my neck, teeth sinking into the soft flesh. "I like it when everyone hears you scream my name." He twisted his wrist in a sharp motion, bringing a fresh flood of pleasure.

"I'll scream as loud as you want, as long as you never stop doing that." I was nearly breathless with need.

He chuckled quietly and compiled, continuing to fuck me with the fingers at a relentless pace. I squirmed against him, hips rocking and bucking, wanting it faster, deeper.

Then Ian rubbed a thumb against my clit and I flew over the edge, shrieking his name. My inner muscles clenched and released, squeezing his fingers. Ian cursed in my ear, a low growl.

"Fuck, sweetness, you're so fucking tight."

I slumped forward against the sink, small jolts of pleasure still shooting through me. My limbs trembled, going weak. The only thing keeping me up was his arm around my waist. Ian slowly withdrew his fingers, inch by inch, drawing a moan from my lips. He gathered me up in his arms and tucked my head under his chin.

I breathed deeply, calming my racing heartbeat.

"You have magic fingers," I murmured against his chest.

He let out a low chuckle. "Lots of practice."

I stiffened.

He mimed playing a riff, air-guitaring in the middle of the bathroom. I laughed, relaxing when I realized what he meant.

I didn't want to think about the other meaning.

I made a motion to pull my dress back up. Ian's hand on mine stopped me.

"Did you think we were done?" His eyes held a wicked glint. He pulled my hips against his, letting me feel his stiff length.

Getting fingered in a bathroom was one thing, but getting fucked in one?

Shivers coursed through me at the thought. Despite the orgasm I'd just experienced at Ian's hand, my hormones were already racing again.

"Maybe you were right," I said.

Ian tilted his head. "About what?"

I gave him a coy smile. "Sometimes it's fun to get dirty."

His eyes lit on fire. His mouth captured mine. When our lips met, I was set aflame. The force of that kiss overwhelmed me. His touch made me forget all about my worries, all about my hang ups. In that moment the only thing that mattered was Ian's skin under my fingers and his firm body against mine.

Ian's tongue traced the seam of my lips. I opened my mouth willingly. Our lips locked in a hot, wet kiss. Our tongues tangled together with passion. His hands explored the curves of my body, running up and down my sides, my front, my back. With an easy tug, my dress fell to the floor along with my panties.

I explored his body in turn, pressing my palms against the hard muscles of his chest, the peaks and valleys of his abs. I played with the soft trail of hair leading me down that tempting V-shape of his lower abdomen, until my fingers reached the waistband of his pants.

I fumbled at his jeans, popping the button open and pulling the zipper down with eager fingers. When his hard cock sprang free I gently took him in my hands. He let out a sharp hiss as I stroked up and down once, twice. He pulled a foil packet out of his pocket and quickly rolled on protection before putting both hands under my thighs.

"Hold onto me," he murmured against my lips.

I wrapped my arms around his neck and my legs around his waist, clinging onto him as he lifted me up. He used his body weight to press me against the wall. His stiff cock pointed upward in the space between our bodies, rubbing against my clit, between my wet folds. I bit my lip to stifle the sounds of pleasure leaving my lips.

He took himself in his hand and used the head to tease at me until I was panting and squirming. He placed his tip just at my entrance, circling it but not entering. I bucked my hips, trying to get him inside. He pulled away a few inches. I groaned in disappointment.

"You need something?" he asked teasingly.

"Yes," I moaned. "Fucking do it."

With a sharp jerk of his hips he slid inside me. I let out a choked sound of pleasure, burying my nails into the skin of his back, clawing at him. I arched my back and tilted my hips, trying to take him deeper.

He gripped the cheeks of my ass in both hands and pulled me closer, grinding our bodies together. I frantically bounced up and down on his cock, riding him. His cock pounded in and out of me. The slickness of my arousal, the clenching of my inner muscles, made him groan. He buried his head in my neck, breathing heavily.

"Fuck. Hope. I can't—"

He reached between our bodies to play with my clit. I threw my head back with a moan of pleasure. I bucked my hips harder, cling to him tighter, urging him on.

"Faster," I gasped. "Harder."

He snapped his hips against mine, penetrating me deeply, fucking me rougher. We found ourselves in perfect rhythm. My climax was getting closer. His cock hardened even further inside me, twitching and pulsing. He slammed into me again and again, hitting that spot. I cried out as I flew over the edge, exploding around him. My whole body trembled with my release.

Ian growled in my ear as he came with me, his own body shaking against mine. His fingers dug into my skin so hard I knew they'd leave bruises. I wanted them to leave bruises. I wanted evidence of this, of how much passion I brought out in Ian. I wanted evidence of how much he wanted me.

When our trembling stopped and we had caught our breath, Ian eased me back down onto the floor. He pressed soft kisses on my lips, my cheeks, my neck.

"That wasn't so dirty, was it?" he asked, a mischievous glimmer in his eyes.

"As far as bathrooms go, this one is pretty clean," I agreed with a tired laugh.

"Cam has a team of house cleaners to take care of that for him."

We pulled our clothes back on and made ourselves presentable again.

"Think that game of Go Fish is still on?" I asked.

"The girls are probably down to their panties by now."

"Then I suppose I'm glad we took this little detour."

Neither of us mentioned the reason why he'd left the game. Neither of us mentioned why I'd come running after him.

Ian had his secrets. Secrets he didn't want to tell me about.

But also secrets he didn't want me to worry about.

I shouldn't want to pry. I shouldn't want to know. It was just a fling, just some fun. None of this was serious. There wasn't any reason to talk about those kinds of things with each other. You didn't divulge your deepest, darkest secrets to the girl you were just casually sleeping with.

I had to keep reminding myself that was all we were. That was all I wanted us to be.

And maybe if I kept on repeating it, I could convince myself that was true.

Chapter 20

Clothes fittings weren't the only thing I was tasked with. My most important assignment was to prepare for Darkest Days' first photoshoot.

Not only did we need pictures of the guys for their album artwork, we needed pictures for promotional purposes. Photos for the website, for social media, for flyers and posters and advertisements — these images were going to be everywhere.

The members were being photographed with their own individual backdrop. We created what was essentially an entire movie set for each of them. You'd think we were filming some Hollywood blockbuster with the level of detail we put into the construction.

Some of the sets had been easier to design than others. Ian and Damon shared the same set — a boudoir-style bedroom with torn sheets and broken glass everywhere.

Cameron's set was split in half — one section styled like the interior of a creepy haunted house for his "demon" side. The other section was styled like the interior of a prince's castle for his "gentleman" side.

The haunted mansion had a sweeping, spiral staircase leading to nowhere. The furniture was covered in fake dusty sheets, as if no one had lived there for years. Candelabras mounted to the walls held black candles, thick blobs of wax melting down the sides. Cobwebs lined every corner. It was as creepy a haunted house as I'd ever seen.

The castle side was something straight out of a Disney movie. The set up had crystal chandeliers, red velvet window dressings, and a gleaming marble floor. It was ready for a prince and princess to have their sweeping dance across the ballroom.

It was similar to some of the rooms in Cameron's own home, minus the empty beer bottles and trash on the floor.

Noah's was more difficult. We created a dark, forbidding forest in the middle of the photography studio. The only time I'd ever seen a tree indoors was during the Christmas season. It was like that multiplied by a dozens.

August's was the worst. My *drowning in tears* concept meant we needed to flood an entire set with several feet of water. I felt bad whenever he shivered, cold and soaking wet. The water couldn't have been warm. He never uttered a word of complaint, though.

We brought in two models to pose with the guys. August and Noah's shoots were solo, but Cameron, Ian and Damon needed to work with a partner in a few of the photos for their concept.

Two gorgeous, leggy women were escorted in. I was immediately self conscious. Their waists were slim, their skin was flawless and their hair had not a strand out of place. I'd been working since six in the morning and my face felt greasy. My own hair had been thrown up in a frazzled bun at the nape of my neck. I felt, and probably looked, like a mess.

I consoled myself that at least I had bigger boobs than they did.

It was fascinating to watch the guys pose for photos, both with the models and by themselves. The photographer would give them directions like, *August, gaze up at the ceiling as if life has no meaning.* The crazy thing was, the guys could do it. The range of emotions they conveyed was impressive. Any one of them could have gone into acting.

I was most impressed with Noah's performance. I'd rarely seen him look anything other than vaguely pissed off. But when he was told to fall to his knees, slump against a tree, and stare into the camera as if he'd rather die than ever open his heart, his face completely changed. His eyes went wide and empty, his expression lost, hopeless.

Then the photographer would finish snapping dozens of photos, give him a satisfied nod, and Noah would go back to being disgruntled.

The last photoshoot for the day was Ian and Damon's. They were both posing with the same girl, one in front of her, the other behind.

Damon was directed to glare at her and pretend he was gripping her arm tight, ready to fling her away. Ian was directed to curl his arm around her waist and place soft kisses to the back of her neck.

He was supposed to *pretend* to kiss her neck, but as I stood behind the photographer and watched the shoot, I saw his lips touch her skin, mouth moving lightly across her jaw, neck, and shoulders.

A slow burn of jealous rage ignited inside me at the sight. My fists clenched at my side, shaking. My lips pressed together in a firm line. The longer the scene went on, the angrier I got. I wanted to look away, but I couldn't tear my eyes off the two of them. It was like watching a train wreck.

Finally, the camera shutter stopping clicking. The photoshoot was done. The model shook out her limbs and stretched. All three of them had been stuck in a similar pose for a while. Damon did the same, rubbing at his neck and groaning.

Ian immediately zeroed in on me. He must have seen the furrow of my brow, the tightness of my lips, my balled fists. He tilted his head and winked.

Jealous? he mouthed.

I whirled around with a huff, turning my back to him. I didn't want him to see me like that. I stalked to the table with catered food and drinks.

I contemplated stuffing my face with food, but remembered Ian's lips all over the thin, slender model. I decided against it. I wasn't hungry anyway.

Two interns brushed by me and filled up their paper plates, sticking to fruits and vegetables.

"Were you watching Noah's photoshoot?" one of them, a blonde girl, asked.

Her friend shook her auburn head. "No, I was too busy watching August." She sighed. "He's so gorgeous."

"Forget it. August would never pay attention to an intern. We're too below him."

"Did you hear that one of those models used to date Damian?"

"Not surprising. I heard they have a thing for models."

"I guess interns are too low on their radar, too."

"I think it's all the same to them. Interns, models, groupies. They see a girl they want, they take her."

"I wish both of them would take me."

They giggled and wandered off, their plates full of rabbit food.

My heart sank to my stomach. Those girls were right. The guys could have anyone they want, including models. Ian probably had more than his fair share of them.

I chided myself internally, shaking off my bad mood. This was what I'd wanted. No strings.

A touch on my waist made me flail.

"Whoa, easy," Ian said. "Why are you so jumpy?"

I forced a laugh. "Sorry. Too focused on the food."

"Is the food that interesting? 'Cause I can think of something else I'd rather devour."

I darted my eyes around, but there was no one close enough to hear.

"In fact," Ian leaned forward, speaking low into my ear, "I know of a private place where we can dine together. Alone."

The press of his lips against my ear caused all breath to leave my lungs.

"We're in the middle of a photoshoot."

"Nope. We're done for the day."

Despite my words, I let him tug me along, leaving the photo area and heading down a deserted hallway housing the studio offices.

"I have to help put stuff away with the other interns."

He pulled me into an empty office and locked the door behind us. "Everyone who showed up at six o'clock has already left. It's the second shift's turn to clean up."

"I still have a lot of work to do to get ready for—" I gasped as Ian bit my ear.

"I know for a fact you don't have anything due for another few days." He mouthed the bite lightly, a soft touch. "You're running out of excuses, sweetheart."

He placed a hand on the small of my back, pressing our hips together. I couldn't help rocking against him.

"Standing next to that girl all day was torture. All I could think about was touching you. Kissing you. Running my hands all over your skin, worshipping every inch of you."

I couldn't believe the line he was giving me.

"Right." I pushed at his chest. "You spent the whole day with a gorgeous model and all you could think about was me."

He pulled me back into the circle of his arms.

"That girl has *nothing* on you, sweetness." He placed a kiss on my cheek. "You're different." He ducked his head until he met my eyes, his own a soft green. "You're special."

Despite my better instincts, I could feel my insides melting, liquid heat flowing to the apex of my thighs.

"How about I prove it to you?" His eyes glinted, playful yet heated. "I'll give you ten kisses for every one I gave her." He lowered his lips to my neck. "I think I kissed her about two dozen times."

"Th-that's a lot of kisses."

"Then I guess I'd better get started."

Ian licked and sucked and nipped at every exposed inch of skin on my neck, shoulders and collarbone.

The press of his teeth, lips, and tongue drove me crazy. I reached up to bury my hands in his hair.

He grabbed my wrists, pinning them against the wall on either side of my head. Trapping me.

"Keep them there."

"But—"

His eyes flashed. "Keep. Them. There."

My heart fluttered. The words were commanding. Powerful. Something inside me flickered to life. Some part of me wanted me to do what he said. Wanted to obey.

I nodded my head to show I understood, not fighting against his hold. His eyes narrowed, humming in satisfaction.

"Good girl."

My knees went weak, a flood of warmth rushing to my very core. I wanted to be good for him. I wanted to please him.

But his own pleasure was the last thing on his mind.

Ian placed soft kisses down my neck, along my collarbone, until he reached the swell of my breasts. As his lips moved downward, his hands slid upward. He untucked my blouse and skimmed along the skin of my stomach. My muscles clenched. His fingers left a blazing hot trail.

Large hands engulfed both breasts. Two thumbs brushed my nipples through the thin cotton bra.

I gasped as a jolt of pleasure went through me. He kissed along my cleavage and massaged with soft touches until I was squirming.

I started to reach down and clutch at his hair. His words echoed in my ears. I clenched my fists instead and kept my arms where he'd placed them.

As if sensing my inner struggle, Ian chuckled darkly. He picked me up with one arm around my hips, the other around my shoulders. Before I knew what was happening, I was sitting on a desk. Ian was between my spread legs. My skirt was bunched up to my waist. I blinked at the suddenness of it.

I didn't have time to protest. Ian went straight for my panties, hooking his fingers under the elastic and tugging. I automatically lifted my hips, not thinking twice. Once my panties were gone, he placed both hands on my inner thighs and spread them obscenely wide.

"Your body is amazing." He murmured the words against the skin of my calf. "I don't think a ratio of ten-to-one is good enough. Let's make it a hundred-to-one."

If anyone walked in, they'd have seen Ian on his knees in front of me, head between my thighs with my legs sprawled out on either side. I should have been embarrassed. I should have been protesting.

Instead, I closed my eyes and whimpered as Ian sucked my clit into his mouth.

He more than made good on his promise.

Chapter 21

By the time Ian was done with me I was a frazzled mess. A frazzled, happy, satisfied mess.

We put ourselves together and went back to the studio. The rest of the band members were gone, but the crew was still taking down all the sets.

"Shit, I missed my ride," Ian said.

"It's your own fault."

"Worth it."

I had to pull myself together and get back to work. "I need to get my purse and stuff."

I could tell he was going to pull me in for a kiss. I side stepped away. I couldn't let him do that in front of everyone.

Ian narrowed his eyes in a fake pout.

"You've manhandled me enough for one day," I admonished. "I'll see you back at Etude."

"Fine. I'll go see if any of the guys are still hanging around somewhere."

I'd misplaced all my things so I had to go looking in every corner and under every table.

I tried to stay out of the way of the crew but I received a few glares when I got too close to a piece of expensive equipment. All those cameras and lights were just waiting for me to bump into them and knock them over.

I still hadn't found my bag. I panicked, wondering if someone had stolen my stuff. I approached one of the interns.

"Hey, have you seen a black leather purse with pointed studs?"

"No, but I think someone complained about our stuff being everywhere," she said. "An assistant moved everything to a break room. The one with the large fridge, not the one with the small water cooler."

Annoying, but better than having it stolen. I thanked her and made my way to the back.

Familiar voices echoed from down the hall. Damon and Ian were there. I was about to push the door open when I heard my name. I paused. The voices got louder, shouting. Damon's voice rang out.

"...hope you know what the fuck you're doing."

"I don't know what you're talking about." Ian sounded as stubborn as Damon usually did.

I should have left. I should have turned around and walked away.

I didn't.

"You know exactly what I'm talking about."

"What do you care, anyway?"

"We fuck them," Damon said bluntly. "We don't fall for them."

"I haven't fallen for her."

"I've seen you two sneak off. I've seen the way she looks at you. You said it was a one-time thing."

"This one is different."

My heart thumped madly in my chest. I peeked through the crack in the door.

"Is the sex that good?" Damon asked sarcastically.

Ian fumed for a brief moment before he smirked. "Man, you've got no fucking idea."

"Listen. I get it, she's hot. I'd fuck her too."

Ian choked, rage exploding across his face. "Don't you even—"

"Then again, maybe not," Damon muttered, talking over his twin. "Those eyes of hers would drive me nuts before too long."

"What's wrong with her eyes?" Ian asked, as a vague feeling of insult spread through my chest.

"I dunno, man. It's like she's gazing into your soul or something. Those concepts she came up with for each of us? Like she's psychic." Damon faked a shudder. "Fucking creepy."

"She's observant."

"Exactly. That's what I'm telling you. She notices things." Damon gave Ian a pointed stare.

Ian's shoulders slumped, as if he were giving up. "It doesn't matter anyway. We're just having fun. She's nothing to me."

My throat closed up. All that stuff he'd said about me being different, about me being special... I'd known it was all just a game to him.

I quickly blinked tears away, admonishing myself. I should have known better. Hasn't I been through this once before? I couldn't believe I'd almost make the same mistake twice.

No more. I wasn't going to let myself fall any further. Whatever I had with Ian was supposed to be fun. Exciting. I shouldn't expect anything other than that. I didn't *want* anything other than that.

"What do you think's going to happen if she finds out?" Damon continued.

Ian flinched. "She won't." He avoided Damon's eyes, playing with the buckles on his wrist brace and twisting it around in circles.

Damon placed his hands over his brother's, tangling their fingers together to stop the fidgeting. "You think she'll just keep quiet about it?"

Ian pulled away with a jerk.

"We did everything we could to keep it a secret," Damon pressed on. "We went on fucking hiatus, Ian."

"She won't find out!"

I'd known the band had gone on hiatus. They never said why. At first fans thought there had been a falling out between the members. When they got back together, we assumed they wanted a break.

They ended their standoff. Damon let out a frustrated growl and stalked towards the door. I quickly fled around a corner, not wanting to get caught.

Damon left the room first. I waited but Ian didn't come out. I tiptoed a few feet down the hallway then made my way back over, shuffling my feet loudly to announce my arrival.

Ian stood in the middle of the room, head bowed, hair falling over his eyes. He was back to fidgeting with his wrist.

"Hey, you still here?" I made my voice purposely cheerful and carefree. I hoped my eyes weren't red-rimmed.

He glanced up with a jolt, his own eyes wide, panicked.

"Sorry!" I said hurriedly. "I didn't mean to startle you. I'm looking for my bag."

He seemed to force himself to relax. "It's okay. I was just lost in thought." He scanned me up and down, a sly grin crossing his lips. "One of your shirt buttons is still undone."

I looked down, horrified to find he was right. How embarrassing. I fumbled to quickly fasten it back up. I hoped no one else had noticed.

He came over and took my hand, squeezing it.

"I forgot to tell you. We're doing a small concert tonight. There's a couple other bands who're going to be playing. You want to come and watch backstage?"

Did he really want me there? Or was he hoping to get a good luck blowjob before he performed?

I pushed back the snide thoughts. I'd known exactly what I was getting into.

"Do I have time to change?"

"Gonna put on sexy little number for me?"

I thought about the clothing currently in my closet. I'd have to borrow from Faith again. "Sure. I'll tart myself up like all the other girls."

He wrapped his arms around my waist and swung me around. I let out a soft shriek.

"You're nothing like the other girls." His eyes sparkled with good humor, but there was something deeper in his voice.

We're just having fun.

Despite the smile on my face, Ian's words were sobering.

She's nothing to me.

I tried to shake it off. It didn't matter. Ian was right. We were just having fun.

Besides, I wasn't going to let myself fall for someone who could break my heart without a second thought.

Still, a small part of me couldn't help snarking.

Too late.

Chapter 22

I hadn't tarted myself up for the concert, but I had at least put on a cute dress I'd borrowed from Faith. It was short, it was tight and it was sexy. I figured that was good enough.

The whole time I got dressed I couldn't help wonder what was the point. Nothing I did was going to make Ian fall for me.

But I didn't want him to fall for me, anyway. We weren't ever going to be anything serious. I'd known that going in. I'd hadn't wanted that. I hadn't wanted any strings. Hadn't planned on getting attached.

I snorted to myself. So much for that.

When I arrived at the concert venue I flashed my ever-present staff badge at the bouncers and was nodded through to the backstage.

I found Ian talking with an assistant, holding his guitar in one hand. He was smiling at her, his head tilted to the side. She was practically swooning. He said something I couldn't hear and she nodded fervently, rushing away to do his bidding. He smirked and slung his guitar over his shoulder.

I tried to ignore the ache in my heart.

Ian noticed me, his eyes lighting up. He headed straight toward me. I braced myself for whatever flirtatious words he was going to say. I got ready to steel my heart against it.

Surprisingly, Ian didn't immediately run and tease me, or flirt with me or put his hands on me.

"This concert is going to fucking rock!" he said with a mad grin. "The fans have been cheering our name for a solid twenty minutes straight already." His eyes twinkled with an almost manic glee. "Can't wait to get on stage."

"What's got you so pumped up?"

"We're going to try out some of our new songs. I can't wait to hear what the audience thinks."

"Are you going to try yours and Damon's song?"

Ian's mouth turned down at the corners, almost seeming to deflate. I immediately regretted asking about it, wondering if it was a sore point.

"Nah." He faked casual shrug. "It's not one hundred percent ready yet. Noah's song is going to rock though." He glanced around the backstage before turning back to whisper. "Honestly, it's such a sappy song I think all the girls in the audience are going to burst into tears."

"Isn't that a good thing?"

"Damon gets pissy at Noah's emotional stuff. Says we want the girls thinking we're sexy rock stars, not some sort of *sensitive artiste*."

"There's nothing wrong with that."

"I thought you were into the rock star god thing? All leather pants and eyeliner, not acoustic guitar and crooning love songs."

"I can enjoy both."

Ian gave me an odd look. "You really like that kind of thing?"

Why do you care what I like? A small, snide voice inside me said. *After all, we're just a fling. I mean nothing to you.*

I pushed aside the pain in my chest.

"I was thinking I might go down to the pit," I told Ian. "Experience the concert firsthand like a real fan, not just watching from backstage."

"And get crushed by a mob of fans? Good luck."

"I am a fan. I'm used to it."

"But you're not a fan anymore. You're working with rock stars, now. You should get to enjoy the perks, like watching backstage without getting trampled on in a mosh pit."

My phone pinged. I suppressed a sigh.

"Sorry. This might be Janet."

"You don't work for her anymore. Tell her to shove off."

"I can't do that."

"Sure you can. Ian snatched my phone from my hand.

"Hey!" I protested.

He looked at the screen. "*Darkest Days' Twin Guitarists Voted Most Eligible Bachelors,*" he read out loud. He looked to me with a raised eyebrow.

I groaned and put my face in my hands.

"This the kind of stuff you usually get notifications on?" He voice held a teasing note.

"Shut up," I grunted.

"You keeping tabs on me?"

"I told you I'm a fan."

Ian put the phone back in my hand. "I'm not sure whether to be flattered or creeped out."

"It's not like I'm stalking you. I need to keep up to date with Darkest Days news for my job."

"News like which member of the band has captured the hearts of women everywhere?"

"It's not my fault that's the kind of news that gets shared online," I grumbled.

"I'll have to blame the media on that one, then." He handed me back my phone with a grin. "You're too cute."

"Ten minutes, guys," August called from near the curtain as he peeked out, surveying the concert hall.

"Give me fifteen," I heard Damon call back with a dark chuckle.

I looked around but couldn't see Ian's brother.

"He's probably getting head from some girl in a dark corner." Ian looked torn between being amused and exasperated. "Don't know why he can't leave the fun for after our concerts." Ian gave me a sly look. "Like the kind of fun we're going to have afterwards."

A lump in my throat made it hard to speak. That's what our whole relationship was about. *Fun.* Two adults having a good time.

"You want to head back to your place after the concert?" I asked.

A pained look crossed his face. "Ah, shit, I forgot." Ian gave me a sorrowful look. "We've got to put in an appearance at a VIP party after the concert. I won't be free for hours."

He genuinely seemed sorry. He actually did want to spend more time with me.

Or maybe he just wanted to spend more time between my legs. The thought sent an unwanted spike of pain through my heart.

This is getting ridiculous, I scolded myself. *Get your feelings under control.*

"I'll make it up to you." Ian traced my lower lip with his thumb, a sensual caress, almost as good as a kiss. My breathed hitched. "Why don't you come over to my place tomorrow night? We can make dinner. Maybe watch a movie."

But from the look in his eyes, I could tell he was imagining a hundred dirty things he could do to make it up to me.

Chapter 23

As I got ready for dinner at Ian's place the next day, a small part of me couldn't help cheering. It was like a date. Maybe he did have feelings for me after all.

My head reminded me that we weren't in a relationship. He wasn't my boyfriend. I certainly wasn't his girlfriend. But my heart wouldn't listen. It still pumped madly at the thought of finally being alone, like a proper couple. Would he cook for me himself? Would there be candles? I was trying to anticipate how romantic the mood might be that evening.

The text messages he sent me all day didn't make it any better. They were half sweet and half dirty.

I've missed spending time alone with you, sweetheart.

There's no better feeling in the world than sinking my cock inside you.

Can't wait to hold you in my arms again.

I'm going to make you come so many times you'll be begging me to stop.

Those texts flustered me in more ways than one. By the time I found myself at Ian's condo apartment I was a bundle of nerves.

"You look amazing." Ian stood in the open doorframe, eyes wandering over my body as if he were a man starved of food and I was a tasty meal. The black bodycon dress I'd borrowed from Faith's closet had been a good choice.

He wore a simple white t-shirt, tight over his chest. His jeans hung low on his hips, practically molded to his legs. When I glanced up, I was met with bright green eyes and a heated stare.

My stomach did flips.

Ian was wrong. He was the amazing one.

"You look good, too." I tried not to sound breathless. I must not have done a good enough job because he tilted his head and smirked. To my relief, he didn't comment.

"Hope you like Italian." He opened the door wide and ushered me in with an arm around my waist.

"I like food in general."

A delicious smell wafted through the air as I entered, tomatoes and herbs.

Ian's condo was a vast open concept space, modern and chic. Cream-colored leather furniture complimented the black and white abstract art on the walls.

His kitchen was off to the side with a large island counter, marble-topped. Four tall barstools in front of it. There was no dining room table.

There were, however, several guitars and amps in a corner near the balcony doors. I went to go touch one before pulling back.

"Are these expensive?"

"A few of them. That one over there was my first." He pointed to one covered in stickers and scuff marks. "It's a piece of shit, but I can't get rid of it."

"Wait, do you play in here?" I asked, aghast. "Don't your neighbors complain?"

"What neighbors? This is the penthouse suite. I have the entire floor to myself."

I glanced around. "It doesn't seem that big."

"I've got a couple extra bedrooms and a small recording studio of my own down that hallway."

I hadn't noticed the hallway. This wasn't an open concept apartment. This whole area was only the living room. I tried to keep my mouth from gaping open. How much did this place cost?

Then again, if Cameron could afford a mansion, why wouldn't Ian be able to afford an entire penthouse right in the heart of downtown?

I wandered over to the far wall to gaze out of the floor to ceiling windows overlooking the city. Everything looked so small from up here. So insignificant.

"You getting overwhelmed?" he teased, wrapping his arms around me from behind.

"A little."

"Soon you'll be able to afford a fancy place like mine."

"Never in my wildest dreams could I afford a place like this."

"You just scored a sweet gig, working as our Image Consultant. Who knows where that might lead?"

"I'm just another intern. You're a famous rock star. I know where I stand."

"You're wrong. We're equals, Hope." He ran a hand through his hair, rueful. "If anything, you're more important than me."

I gave him a skeptical look. "You can't possibly think that."

"Do you know how many musicians are out there waiting to be discovered? Believe me, if I quit music tomorrow, they'd find a replacement within minutes."

"You're underestimating how much people love you."

"They love *Damian*. They love the idea of The Twins. No one cares about Ian."

My heart clenched, aching for him. "I care about Ian."

His eyes flicked up to mine, examining me closely, as if trying to discern whether I was lying or not. I don't know what he saw in my eyes, but he pulled me forward, brushing his lips against mine, a not-quite kiss.

"That's why you're different," he murmured into my mouth. "That's why you're special."

Those pretty words again. I'd come to both love them and loathe them.

I wanted to hear more.

I wanted him to stop saying them.

I wanted to believe he meant them.

I knew better than to hope he was telling the truth.

I stepped away from the circle of his arms, giving myself space. "What are we having for dinner?"

He tugged me close again, our fronts pressed together. "I know what I'm having for dinner."

The wicked grin he gave me made my stomach do flips.

"We don't want dinner to get cold."

"It'll keep," he dismissed. "Right now there's something I want even more."

"How about we save that for after?" I didn't know if I wanted to have sex while my feelings were still so tangled up.

Ian almost pouted. It was cute.

"After, then," he agreed.

The food was simple but delicious. Fresh, handmade pasta dressed in light olive oil and parmesan sauce with diced tomatoes. I had to keep myself from moaning when I took my first bite.

"This is amazing. Did you make it?"

Ian laughed. "Hell no. I have no idea how to use half the gadgets in my kitchen. I ordered in. I can make bacon, pancakes, sometimes omelets, and ramen noodles. That's it."

"*Sometimes* omelets?"

"It usually ends up being scrambled eggs."

"It's good to be aware of one's strengths and weaknesses."

"And you? Can you cook?"

"I sort of had to learn how. My dad worked all the time so my sister and I took turns after my mom—" I cut myself off and looked down, twirling the pasta with my fork.

Ian put his hand on mine. "Is she...?"

"She passed away when I was young. Car accident."

He spun me around on the rotating chair to face him. "I'm sorry. I didn't mean to bring up bad memories."

"It's okay. It was a long time ago."

He must have recognized the pained look on my face. "Even though it was a long time ago, that kind of thing never really heals."

"It wasn't just her death. It was—" I cut myself off. I didn't want to ruin the evening with my teenaged angst.

"You can tell me." Ian's voice was so sincere.

I debated for long moments. I hadn't confessed my feelings like this to anyone before. I'd never had anyone I felt comfortable enough unloading on. It wasn't exactly a pleasant conversation starter. But Ian had always listened to me, even in the beginning. He seemed to genuinely care. Maybe I could trust him. Maybe he would understand.

"After losing mom, our dad just kind of... stopped. I don't think he ever recovered. He spent all his time working. He was never home, and when he was it was like Faith and I weren't even there. I think... he couldn't stand the sight of us. We reminded him too much of our mother."

"I'm sorry."

"It's okay. I'm over it. We grew up, moved out and moved on." I blinked back the sting of tears at the back of my eyes. "So Faith and I have only each other to rely on. We've always had each other's backs."

"It's good to have a sibling help you get through the hard times."

Ian appeared startled at himself and glanced away.

"Has Damon helped you through stuff?" I asked carefully.

He was silent for a moment before lifting one shoulder in a casual shrug.

"Just the usual bullshit that comes with being famous. You know."

I didn't know. But I wanted to.

"You guys went on hiatus, right? Did that have something to do with it?"

Ian stiffened. "Why would you think that?" he said slowly.

"Just curious." I tried to play it off lightly. "Some of the other interns were talking the other day. I was wondering. I remember reading about it in the news."

"We needed a break."

"Is that all?"

"Yeah."

I wasn't satisfied with that answer, but I knew it was the only one I was going to get.

He stood abruptly. "I'm going to go get us dessert."

I watched his retreating back as he headed into the kitchen.

Ian had secrets. Secrets he obviously didn't want to share with me. And why would he? I wasn't anyone special. I wasn't his confidant. I was just the girl he was sleeping with.

It was obvious I would never be anything more.

My phone buzzed. A welcome distraction. I peeked at it. Another Darkest Days update.

The screen displayed an entire gallery of the guys at different parties. In every photo they had their arms around a woman. Sometimes multiple women.

My eyes were drawn to the photos of Ian and Damon. On that small screen, I couldn't tell who was who. There were a handful of pictures where they were locking lips with some girl.

I didn't want to believe it was Ian. I couldn't. He was different. Ian thought *I* was different. There was a real connection between us. But it wasn't true, was it?

The sweet things Ian said had gotten to me. Made me think maybe we had something more. But they were no doubt the same words he said to every girl to get them into bed.

I thought I could do it. I thought, if I went in with my eyes wide open, I could get involved with Ian without getting attached.

But from the way my heart ached at seeing those pictures, I'd long lost that battle.

My phone buzzed again.

"I know that's not me texting. You got another guy on the side?" Ian's voice came from behind me, light and teasing.

"It's my sister." I skimmed her text.

Guess who I ran into again? Mr. All-Girls-Drop-Their-Panties-For-Me.

What? Where?

My boss had some meeting at your company. Talking about some launch party, I dunno. I nearly kicked him in the balls.

Lips pressed to the back of my neck. I inhaled a sharp breath.

"Faith sounds feisty," Ian said, continuing to place kissed along my exposed throat.

I held my phone to my chest. "It's not polite to read someone's private text messages."

"But what if it wasn't your sister? What if it was another guy sexting you? I might have to get jealous."

A sharp stabbing pain shot through my chest. I pulled away. "Stop."

"Stop what?" He tugged me back against his chest. "Stop this?" He latched onto my neck, giving me a sucking kiss.

Stop pretending you care.

I didn't voice the words aloud. I didn't want him to think I was falling for him like all his other fangirls and groupies. It would probably give him great satisfaction to know he was starting to get to me. That's what Ian did. Made you fall for him, then left you for the next girl.

"Maybe I need to send you a few more messages to make sure," he continued, lifting his lips from my throat.

"Make sure what?"

"Make sure you remember exactly what I can give you that other men can't."

"And what is that, exactly?"

I felt the wicked curve of his lips against my neck. He slid his hand down my front to the heat between my legs.

Sex. That was it. It certainly wasn't anything else.

It certainly wasn't love.

Ian's fingers caressed the valley of my panties, tracing the folds he'd been buried inside numerous times before. The ache between my legs didn't come close to the ache in my chest.

I couldn't do this anymore.

I removed his arm and stood up, walking a few feet away to give myself space. I kept reminding myself I had known what I was getting into. No commitment. No expectations. Ian and I were just having fun, and that's it. There I'd been, thinking about some sort of romantic evening, when all Ian expected was casual sex.

It was one thing to like Ian, to be attracted to him, to have a fangirl crush on him. It was another thing entirely to start developing real feelings when I knew he would never return them. That was unacceptable.

I wasn't going to let myself fall any further. I wasn't going to wait for him to break my heart.

"I think we should stop."

He tilted his head, confused. "Stop what? Stop sexting?" He cracked a grin. "You worried someone's going to read my filthy messages?

"No. I mean, I think we should stop... this."

Ian's eyes grew wide and confused.

"Our fling," I clarified.

He was stunned for a moment before shaking his head, chuckling. "You can't mean you're breaking up with me."

He honestly thought the idea was absurd. Of course. It was always the rock star who did the dumping.

"It's not a break up. You said it yourself. This is just a fling."

"But.... Why?" He was utterly astounded.

I couldn't tell him the real reason. That I was starting to fall for him. That I knew he would never feel the same. "I just think it's time."

Ian clamped his mouth shut, jaw muscles twitching. His eyes flicked away, avoiding mine.

"Let's just go back to the way things were," I told him. "You can keep on partying and flirting and bringing girls home."

And I'll continue bringing myself off, alone, to thoughts of you.

He rubbed at his wrist cuff again, fidgeting, like a nervous habit. I held my breath, wondering how he was going to react.

"You're right," he said after a long moment. "Maybe it's time we ended things."

A jab of pain went right through my heart. I'd hoped...

But no. Of course he wouldn't ask me to stay. I was just a fun distraction to him.

"So. This is it?" Ian met my gaze, green eyes shuttered.

"Yeah. Let's forget it ever happened and continue working together as colleagues. I don't want things to be awkward."

The muscles in his jaw shifted again, as if he were biting back words. His fists clenched at his sides. He must have always been the one to break it off. He probably had no idea how to react.

"We agreed, remember? We can handle this like adults."

Ian stared at me for several seconds, as if he were seeing straight through me. "Right. Like we agreed." After several more long moments, he glanced away, not meeting my eyes.

I slowly grabbed my purse from a side table and edged towards the door. "So. I guess I'll see you tomorrow?"

"Yeah."

He was still turned away. Was I the first person to have ever called it off?

"Goodnight, Ian."

"Bye." He wouldn't look at me.

I closed the door behind me softly.

The further I got from his apartment, the stronger the ache in my chest grew. I forced myself to ignore it.

I wasn't kidding myself. As much as I wished it were otherwise, I'd known what we had was temporary. I'd done the right thing by calling it off before things went too far.

But somewhere deep inside, I could feel my heart shattering anyway.

Chapter 24

Ian's ego must have taken a huge blow. Being the one broken up with, and not the other way around, had clearly effected him.

I hadn't wanted things to be awkward between us. That was wishful thinking. He'd been avoiding me ever since our "break up." He barely glanced at me when we were in the same room together. From the way he acted, it was like no girl had ever turned him down before.

He didn't seem angry with me. He simply didn't acknowledge my presence. Whenever I directed a question at him, Damon answered, pretending to be his brother.

I had expected Ian to shrug and tell me something flippant like, *it was fun while it lasted.* But instead, he had quietly agreed and then proceeded to deny my very existence.

Or maybe that's what he did whenever he dumped a girl. Maybe he stopped caring entirely.

We're just having fun.

She's nothing to me.

The memory of Ian's words made my throat close up. I didn't expect things would be like this when I broke it off. I expected Ian and I could still be, if not friends, at least on friendly terms with each other.

It turned out, I really did mean nothing to him in the end.

"You sure you want to sit in on this?" one of the assistants asked me. "It's going to be the same old questions they're always asked."

The band was scheduled to appear on a local talk show to promote their new album. It wasn't finished yet, but the marketing department decided to get ahead of promotions. They wanted fans excited before releasing a single song.

I tagged along because I wanted to see them in action, so to speak, when they talked to the DJ. Every person acts slightly different depending on the situation, whether signing autographs for fans, performing on stage, or talking to the media. I needed to know more about Darkest Days to make sure I was getting the concepts right. I needed to make sure the concepts really fit with their personalities.

My mind threatened to drift to Ian again. My chest began to ache. I viciously yanked my thoughts back to the present.

I took note of my surroundings to distract myself. The radio studio was like a police station interview room from a TV show. There was a table in the middle of the room with a chair on one side and a second chair across from it. The wall nearest the door had a one-way mirror. It was cold and sterile, aside from the microphones and other recording equipment on the table.

"You sure it's a radio interview and not an interrogation?" I muttered.

Another assistant shot me a glare, shushing me as she walked by with an extra chair under her arm. She set a group of five chairs around the table so the band could sit comfortably. I'd arrived early with the others. The radio host was nowhere to be seen.

There was a commotion in the hallway. The band had arrived. I resisted the urge to duck behind one of the other interns. I didn't need to. I was on the other side of the recording room, behind the one-way mirror. The guys couldn't see me through the glass.

They were dressed up as if they were ready to go on stage. Odd, considering it was a radio interview. No one would see what they looked like. I noticed a few people snapping pictures here and there, and then it made more sense. The PR and social media team would no doubt be posting pictures of this interview all over the internet.

Cameron was the only one dressed sort of normal — or as normal as Cameron could get, which simply meant he was wearing a t-shirt to go along with his dark denim and decorative chains. His bright red hair was wild as ever, strands falling over his face, nearly obscuring his kohl-smudged eyes.

Black skinny jeans and a white t-shirt was August's usual outfit. Platinum blond hair was tied at the back of his neck. Despite the loose hair that kept falling out of his short ponytail and into his face, his thoughtful expression didn't falter into annoyance once.

Noah had slung his ever-present leather jacket over his shoulder instead of wearing it. The tight black t-shirt fit him well, although the dark color hid the toned abs all fangirls squealed over during their rare appearance.

Ian and Damon walked in last, green eyes flashing with mirth at something Cameron said. A spike of painful desire speared my heart. Heat flooded through my body, centering between my legs.

Every. Single. Time. The longer I went without being in Ian's presence, the more I forgot how much power he had over me. Then I would see him again and be reminded. Vividly.

I fought to put my feelings aside and simply observe. The Twins both wore matching Metallica shirts and faded jeans ripped at the knees. Their hair was styled up, spiked, but still seemed soft to the touch.

I knew exactly how soft Ian's hair was. I'd run my hands through it countless times while he'd kissed me. While he'd touched me. While he'd been inside me.

My thighs clenched together at the flood of memories.

Why exactly had I called it off again?

Ian's eyes flickered around the room, as if seeking something. He glanced at the mirror and stopped. He was staring right at me. He couldn't see me, could he? The glass only went one way. My breath caught in my throat as I met his green eyes.

This. This was exactly why I'd called it off. One look and I was ready to melt. One look and my heart throbbed with longing.

I made the right choice, I told myself. *None of it was real. It was just sex.*

And that's all it was ever going to be.

"Glad you all could make it." The radio DJ walked in a few seconds after the band members took their seats. She wore a plain navy shift-style dress but was well accessorized with thin silver and gold necklaces around her neck and matching bracelets.

I wondered if she always dressed up for work, or if this was because she was interviewing a famous rock group.

She appeared tired with bags under her eyes, which explained the extra large coffee she carried.

I watched with the other assistants and interns behind the mirror as she shook hands with them all and made her greetings.

"Nice to meet you all. My name's Tonya." She sat and took a huge gulp of her coffee before continuing. "If you don't mind, I'll go over a few of the questions I'll be asking, so we can make sure the interview goes off without a hitch."

"Our manager sent over a list of questions you're to ask us." August gave Tonya a pointed stare.

"Yes, I've read them. I won't go off script too much, but sometimes interviewee answers take us to interesting places. If we're veering too close to a subject you don't wish to talk about, let me know."

Cameron leaned over and whispered something to Noah, who let out a small snort.

"Mostly I'll be asking about your new album," she continued. "Your inspirations, where you got your ideas, things like that. Noah, I'll also be asking about the meaning of the lyrics. You're the main lyricist, right?"

Noah nodded shortly.

"And August, you're the main composer?"

"That's right. Although we all work together to finalize every piece."

"Actually, each of us has worked on individual songs," Cameron said, "so there's at least one written and composed solely from each member on this album."

Tonya's eyes lit up. "I'll be sure to ask each of you about that." Her eyes shifted to a digital clock on the wall counting down and hurriedly took another few mouthfuls of coffee. "We'll be on air in about thirty seconds. Put on your earphones and sit closer to the microphones."

The band arranged themselves in time for the ten second mark. The on-air light flipped on. Tonya immediately broke out into a huge smile as she spoke into the microphone and introduced her guests. The smile made her voice sound cheerful and wide awake. Maybe that was her own version of fake-it-til-you-make-it.

"So fellas," Tonya asked, bright and chipper. "First things first. Why don't you say hello to your fans who are listening. Our social media feed exploded when we announced you'd be on."

"Our fans are the absolute best," Cameron said. He leaned into the microphone. "You hear that guys? We wouldn't be here if it weren't for you. We love each and every one of you."

"I can practically hear the screams from here," Tonya said. "You just set aflame the hearts of a hundred girls."

"Only a hundred?" Cameron sounded insulted.

"You're lucky if it's a hundred," Noah muttered, his arms folded over his chest. Cameron made a face at him.

"Is that why you always strip on stage?" Tonya asked. "To appease your fans?"

"Nothing makes girls cream in their panties more than a shirtless guy in jeans. And I would know." He gave a smug grin.

Tonya moved on smoothly, "let's talk about your new songs. I've heard it's a concept album. Can you tell us a little bit about it?"

"The theme of the album is the rise and fall of a relationship," August answered. "From first love, to passionate sex to heartbreak."

"And the album was a team effort?"

"We all worked together closely to make it the best we could," Damon answered.

"Noah, how do you feel about singing other people's lyrics?"

"It's fine."

Cameron nudged him with an elbow. Noah grumbled quietly, but sat up and answered.

"The words don't need to be written by me. It's fine as long as I can understand the meaning behind them. The guys and I have worked together for a long time. When I read the words they've written, I can feel the truth of their feelings in my heart."

It was such a poetic thing to say. It was also the most I'd heard Noah speak. His gravelly voice sounded as erotic in person as it did on stage.

"Cameron mentioned before the interview each member wrote a song themselves. August, did you find it difficult to write lyrics?" Tonya continued. "You're mainly the composer, yes?"

"Lyrics aren't my strong point," August admitted. "It took me a while to figure out what I wanted to say."

"And what is that, exactly?" Tonya pressed.

"You'll find out when the album is released."

"Fair enough. Cameron, what about you?"

"Writing my own song was so much fun. Although August made me take out all the really dirty words, that jerk. He wouldn't even let me say fuc—"

Noah clamped a hand over Cameron's mouth.

"Remember boys, we *are* on public radio."

"And then we've got The Twins," Cameron continued. "Their song rocks."

"You two wrote your song together?" Tonya asked.

"We did," Ian answered, leaning forward into the microphone. "My brother and I wrote these awesome dueling guitar solos. The fans are gonna go crazy over it."

"I thought each of you worked on a single song yourselves," Tonya asked.

"The Twins are basically one person anyway," Cameron said.

Ian froze, his shoulders tensing up.

"Why didn't you each write your own song?" Tonya asked.

"*Damian* wrote the song," Damon said.

"That's what we call those two." Cameron jerked a thumb at both of them. "Damon and Ian."

"And which one is which?" Tonya asked.

"Doesn't matter." Damon chuckled. "Like Cam said, we're practically the same person."

Ian turned away. His eyes almost met mine through the mirror again before they flicked away, a pained expression on his face.

A beep sounded in the room and Tonya glanced at the clock quickly. "It looks like it's time for a commercial break. We'll be back in a few minutes with more questions for Darkest Days." Tonya took off her headset and shook out her hair. "Great job so far. You've got a few minutes."

The guys got up from their seats and stretched their limbs. Ian made a beeline for the door. It caught my attention, but no one else noticed. Damon was distracted by Cameron making a wisecrack, joining in with the laughter.

I got the urge to follow him, but stopped myself. So what if Ian was upset? So what if no one else noticed? It wasn't my business anymore. Whatever it was, he could handle it himself.

But Damon and Ian's voice kept echoing in my ears.

We did everything we could to keep it a secret.

She won't find out!

Worry filled my chest. I remembered what I'd asked him that night at his apartment, before I'd broken it off.

Has Damon helped you through stuff?

Just the usual bullshit.

But Damon's attention was elsewhere. He hadn't noticed his brother run off.

And that look I'd seen on Ian's face...

You should go after him, August had said at Cameron's party. *Don't let him be alone.*

I bolted from my chair and ran.

Chapter 25

Ian had almost disappeared down the hallway. I was about to call out to him when he slipped into the men's washroom. I hesitated. Maybe he wasn't upset after all? Maybe he really just needed a break. I still wanted to talk to him and make sure he was okay. I waited.

Swearing and cursing came through the washroom door. Ian's voice. I paused for a brief moment — this was the men's washroom, after all — before pushing open the door. I hoped there was no one else inside. That would be beyond awkward. There was row of stalls and empty urinals. I turned the corner to find Ian standing in front of the mirror over the sinks.

My heart stopped.

Ian's fingers were covered in blood. He pressed a wad of paper towel to his lower arm, near the back of his wrist. His whole body was shaking. The counter was smeared with red. My breath hitched, echoing loudly among the tiled walls.

He whirled around. His eyes were wide and glassy. The expression on his face went from shock, to shame, to anger, all within seconds.

"Get out," he snarled. He pressed harder on his wrist.

I realized what this was, what Ian was doing. It was like a blow to my chest.

"Ian..." I couldn't make myself say anything other than his name.

He growled and whirled around, shoulders hunched over. "I'm fine. The hand dryer had a sharp edge. That's all."

My heart nearly burst out of my chest with a dozen emotions. Fear, worry, nausea. I struggled to push them aside. The last thing Ian needed right now was for me to freak out. I slowly pulled a handful of paper towels from the dispenser and folded them over. I approached from behind on uneasy feet.

"Let me see." I kept my voice steady and purposely soft. He yanked his arm away when I reached for it.

"I told you to get out."

I placed a hand on his back and felt him shaking. "It's okay. Let me help."

"I don't need your help." But despite his words he seemed to deflate, all fight going out of him. I took his limp arm and pulled away the wad of blood-soaked paper.

I winced. A long, thin cut on the back of his arm. Perfectly straight, no jagged edges. It was deep. I was sure it went deeper than he'd planned.

I kept my voice to a near whisper. "Was it a razor blade?"

He swallowed, a thick sound, before taking in a shaky breath. He nodded silently.

I placed the fresh wad of paper towel over the wound and pressed. Ian hissed, jerking away reflexively. I held on, not letting him go.

We were both quiet for long moments, me with my head bowed over his injured arm, him with his face turned away. He stared at the door like he was contemplating making a run for it.

I took his other hand and pressed it over the cut in place of mine. I wet another handful of paper and cleaned his hands and the sink, wiping away the streaks of blood.

"How long has this been going on?"

He didn't answer. Instead, he peeled off the paper towel and showed me.

Dozens of thin scars with ridged skin, silvery-pink. One single line of scabbed over skin. It couldn't have been more than a few weeks old.

"That time I saw you coming from the washroom. This is what you were doing?"

His hands trembled. I glanced up to meet his eyes, still glassy. From pain? From endorphins?

"You can't tell anyone."

"Ian..."

He grabbed my shoulders with both hands, paper towel fluttering to the floor. The wound had stopped bleeding, but it still looked painful. "Promise me you won't tell anyone. *Please*. If August finds out, he'll make me quit."

Did he mean quit the band, or quit cutting himself?

Ian clutched at me desperately. "*Promise me.*"

I tried to speak in soothing tones, tried to reason with him. "You need to get help."

"I already got help!" He let me go, storming away the few paces he could in the small washroom. "We already went on hiatus once. We can't do it again."

"Maybe that's what you need."

"No." Ian's lips were firm, his eyes resolute. "You don't get to make that choice for me."

"Someone clearly has to."

Ian shook his head vehemently. He shoved his hand inside his pants pocket and pulled out a pad of white gauze. He'd been prepared. How often did he do this? He folded it over into a rectangle, thick but narrow. He pressed it to his arm with one hand and took his wrist cuff from the sink with the other.

"No one needs to know."

He put the cuff back on, buckling the straps tight. It completely hid the scars and pressed the gauze over the wound. It would scab over underneath the leather. He was going to hide it from everyone. He was going to go out there and pretend everything was fine.

"At least talk to your brother." Damon would know what to do. Right?

"What do you care, anyway?"

Tears stung my eyes. A vice squeezed my lungs. "I care. Of course I care."

"We're just a fling, remember?" He threw the words back in my face, sharp and biting.

"I can't sit back and watch while you hurt yourself."

He stared straight through me, expression blank, but I could see the distress in his eyes. "Then I guess it's a good thing you don't have to."

He turned his back on me and walked out.

I stared at the swinging door for long moments. Then I began cleaning up the few red drops in the sink with soap and water. I was on autopilot, my brain going a million miles an hour.

She won't find out! Ian had told his brother.

But I had.

Ian cut himself.

Doctors called it self-harm. The cuts weren't on the inside of his wrist. They were on the back of his arm. And not one or two. He must have been doing it for years.

Why? What would make someone do that to themselves?

Despite Ian's plea, there was no way I could keep it a secret. Not something as big as this.

I cleaned up the last of the paper towels and flushed them down the toilet. On the way out of the stall I caught my reflection in the mirror. My face was pale, my eyes wide, full of worry and fear. My hair was more frazzled than usual.

The two minute break was more than over by the time I gathered myself together. The interview was already done. The band members were getting ready to leave.

I kept my eyes trained on Ian. He seemed... fine. Perfectly normal. There was no hint of that glassy look. It had been replaced by an amused glint as he laughed along with something Cameron said. He was so good at pretending. If I hadn't walked in on him, I probably never would have known.

And how could I? This was the last thing I would expect from Ian. From any of the guys.

A drinking problem, maybe. Drugs, even. He was a rock star after all. It wasn't uncommon.

But self-harm?

Damon and Ian both saw me, a quick glance. Ian whispered something to his brother. Damon listened for a brief moment before throwing a withering glare my way. Damon slowed his steps. He whispered something back and nodded to his brother, indicating he should go on ahead.

Ian gave him a warning look and touched his arm. Damon shook it off with an easy smile that didn't quite reach his eyes. Ian continued walking with the rest of the band. Damon stood and watched him for a few seconds. Then he whipped around and met my gaze head on.

I froze in my tracks.

Damon stalked over. There was nothing easy or casual in that stride. He stopped within two feet of me. It was like the first time The Twins had noticed me backstage. Except that time, I hadn't been terrified for my life.

"So." Damon's lip curled in displeasure. "You found out?"

I almost couldn't make myself speak. "You mean, about the..."

Damon hissed, eyes darting around to see who was within hearing distance. "Shut up!"

I snapped my mouth shut.

He let out a frustrated growl and ran his fingers through his hair. "I told Ian this would happen." Damon stared me down with narrowed, chilling eyes. I shrank back.

"You better not tell a soul."

"I-I won't."

"Good."

The corners of his lips tilted up. It wasn't friendly, or reassuring.

"Because if word gets out, I will fucking *destroy you.*"

Chapter 26

I was still trembling by the time I got back home, adrenaline still pumping through my veins. I barely managed to kick off my shoes before I fled to my room and slammed the door behind me. As if hiding in the sanctuary of my bedroom would protect me.

Damon's words echoed my head, a never ending litany.

He said he would destroy me.

The back of my eyes stung with unshed tears. I'd never had someone direct so much hatred towards me. It was scary.

But the terror was soon replaced with rage.

Damon knew.

Damon *knew*. He knew Ian was hurting himself, and he wasn't doing anything about it.

I was angry beyond reason, ready to smash something, anything. I kicked my laundry basket over, punched at my pillows until they were lumpen and misshapen.

But eventually my anger deflated.

I couldn't stay mad at Damon. After all, I knew about Ian's problem now, too, and I hadn't done anything about it. I should have told August the minute I found out. Instead, I'd run home, scared.

Ian didn't want anyone to know. His brother was no doubt simply obeying his wishes.

Maybe I should do the same. Ian was an adult. I had no say in how he lived his life.

But if I didn't say anything, and Ian ended up really hurting himself, if he ended up—

I couldn't finish the thought.

If Ian ended up seriously injured, I didn't know if I'd be able to live with myself.

I had to tell someone. But the look on Ian's face, the fear I'd seen, made me think twice. I didn't want to betray him.

I didn't know what to do.

There was a knock on my door.

"Hope?"

My sister's voice was full of worry. I hadn't known she was home, or I would have tried to be more quiet.

I wanted to tell her. I wanted to confide in her. She was so smart, so level headed.

I opened the door.

"Are you crying?" Faith immediately pulled me into a hug, squeezing me tight. "What happened? Are you okay?"

"I'm fine," I mumbled in his her shoulder. "I was just..."

I didn't know what to tell her.

She urged me into the bedroom. When we were both sitting on the bed, she took my hand. "Whatever it is, you can tell me."

I rubbed at my red-rimmed eyes with a fist and shook my head.

"We haven't had much time to talk lately," she said quietly. "We used to talk about everything. About anything."

"We've been busy. The both of us. You've got all these events, I've got this internship."

I still hadn't told her about my promotion to Image Consultant. Faith was right. We'd barely spoken in months. I'd missed her.

"Can you tell me why you were crying?" she asked. "Is it about a guy?"

She probably thought I was heartsick over some guy I'd slept with. And I was. But not in the way she imagined.

"I found out something about a friend. He's in trouble. I want to help, but I don't know how."

"What kind of trouble?" She sat up, alarmed. "Is it drugs?"

"No. Nothing like that." I tried to give her a reassuring smile.

"So if it's not drugs, what is it?"

"I want to tell you but I'm not sure it's my place."

"What *can* you tell me?"

I paused for a moment, thinking. "I found out a secret. Something he doesn't want anyone else to know. But if I don't tell someone, I'm afraid he'll get hurt."

That was close enough to the truth.

"Hurt? Hurt like how?"

I couldn't tell her.

"Hurt bad enough I'm worried for his safety." Worried for his life. "But I don't think he'll ever forgive me if I told."

Faith squeezed my hand. "I guess it comes down to what's more important. Is his safety more important than his feelings for you? Are you willing to watch him get hurt just so he won't be upset with you?"

I shot off the bed. "Of course not! His safety is the only thing that matters."

"Then I guess you know what you have to do."

My shoulders slumped. "It's not that easy. I don't want to betray his trust."

She pursed her lips. "Well. You don't necessarily need to be the one who tells."

"What do you mean?"

"He's in trouble. Even though he doesn't want anyone to know, I'm sure deep down inside somewhere he's desperate for help. You need to convince him. Get him to ask for help so you don't have to go behind his back."

I stared at her for a few minutes before throwing my arms around her shoulders. "How do you always know what to say?"

"That's what sisters are for."

I pulled back and wiped the tears from my cheeks. "Thanks."

I hoped she was right. I had to talk to Ian. I had to make him understand. To convince him to get help.

And if that didn't work, if Ian didn't agree to tell someone...

I pushed those thoughts aside, not wanting to get ahead of myself. Talk to Ian first. Then decide what to do.

Faith took my hand. "Hope... can I assume Mr. Sexting is the one you're talking about?"

I stiffened, but then remembered she didn't know who he was. "Yeah. It's him."

Worry flickered across her face. "I just need to ask. Are you sure? I don't want you to be making a mistake, getting involved with this guy."

"So what if I am? It's my mistake to make."

"What if he hurts you?"

"Then I guess I'll have to live with a broken heart."

And there it was. I finally admitted it to myself, the words I'd been avoiding.

I was in love with Ian.

Even if he would never love me back, even if I meant nothing to him, it didn't change my feelings. I would help him, whether he wanted me to or not.

"Is he really worth it?"

Flashes of Ian's face flicked across my vision, echoes of his words in my ears.

You keep up the good work, sweetheart.

Does the princess need more wooing from her prince?

Tell me you want this. Tell me you want me.

"Yes. He is."

Chapter 27

"Ian, please, let me in."

I pounded my fist against the door, the loud hammering matching the pounding in my heart.

I'd begun to think he wasn't home. Or maybe he was still as determined to ignore me now as he had been since I'd ended things. I was getting discouraged. Discouraged and worried. What if he was hurting himself again? What if he was doing it right now, while I was stuck outside? I let out a sick choking sound, an almost sob.

"Ian, *please!*"

The door finally swung open a crack, my fist inches away from another heavy knock.

I pushed through to find Ian already heading back to his sofa. He flopped onto the cushions and faced me.

"What? What do you want?"

Even with a sullen expression, even with his tired eyes, he was still as gorgeous as he was the first time I'd seen him on stage. More so in his vulnerability.

I spoke softly, trying not to spook him. "I wanted to talk."

"Nothing to talk about," he muttered.

"You know there is."

I sat beside him gingerly on the opposite end of the couch, leaving space between us. I didn't want to crowd him.

"I can't forget what I saw today."

"Yes you can. You have to."

"I'm worried. You're hurting yourself. What if next time—"

"There won't be a next time!" he shouted, flinging himself off the sofa. Then he stopped and ran a hand over his face. "...probably."

"You've been doing it for years."

"That was a long time ago."

"You did it a few weeks ago."

"A momentary relapse."

"Then what was today?"

He went quiet.

"You need help," I begged. "You have to tell someone."

"I *can't.*" His eyes were desperate, wild. "*Please.* You're the only one who knows, aside from my brother. It has to stay that way." Ian must have sensed my anger. "Don't blame Damon."

"He threatened me if I told anyone."

Ian glanced away, ashamed. "He doesn't know I've started up again," he confessed quietly. "He thinks you saw my old scars." His eyes flicked to mine. "It's no one's fault. This is all me. It's how I deal with things."

"You call this dealing?"

"Look, it's nothing."

I gestured at his arm. "That isn't nothing, Ian."

"I've been good for years."

"Then why are you carrying a razor blade around?"

He lips quirked up, half-amused, half-ashamed. "Security blanket." Ian caught my failing arms and held my wrists in his one good hand. "I only did it once recently before today. I forgot how to do it properly and went a little too deep this time. I promise, you don't have to worry."

Tears filled my eyes. "You're hurting yourself. How can I not worry?"

His tried to give me a reassuring smile, but it looked sickly. "It's not like I'm suicidal. I only do it on the back of my arms."

"That doesn't make it any better."

"I'm just saying. I'm not going to kill myself."

"Then *why?* Why do it?"

Ian let out a deep breath and collapsed back onto the sofa. "It's hard to explain."

"Tell me." This time I sat close, knees tucked under me, pressing my thighs against his. "I want to understand."

Ian leaned forward, elbows on his knees, the heels of his hands pressed over his eyes. For a long moment, I didn't think he was going to answer. Then he spoke.

"Growing up... our dad was pretty shitty. At first it was just cruel words. Putting us down all the time. He made us feel worthless. Then came the yelling, the anger. Then came the hitting, the beatings."

I leaned my head on his shoulder and placed one hand on his chest. I didn't say anything, just let him talk.

"Our mom was so cowed. So beaten down. She didn't do a thing to stop it. I don't think she could, mentally or emotionally. She tried to pretend everything was okay, living in her own little world. But nothing was okay."

"I'm sorry."

He let out a heavy breath, going silent for a moment.

"The cutting made it better," he finally admitted.

I scooted back so I could meet his eyes. "How?"

"I think..." he trailed off thoughtfully. "I think it's almost like it took all the hurt and anger and pain that I was feeling inside and made it physical. The pain on the outside made the pain on the inside feel less terrible. I guess you could call it a coping mechanism." He let out a dark laugh. "Pretty awful coping mechanism, I know."

My brow furrowed. "But... how did Damon not know?"

"I kept it from him for a long time. We weren't always as close as we are now. Our dad played us against each other. It didn't exactly make for warm fuzzy feelings between us."

"I never would have guessed. You seem inseparable now."

"That started when Damon found out. When he finally discovered what I was doing, he was determined to help me. He watched me like a hawk. He was there to snap me out of it when I started spiraling down. He was there for me whenever I needed him."

"But you still continued to cut, even with his help?"

"I stopped for a long time. I thought I'd stopped for good. That it was behind me."

"But something must have gone wrong a few years ago. It must have been bad. You went on hiatus."

Ian nodded, playing with a strand of my hair. "We did."

"Can I ask what happened?" I was hesitant, still not sure how much he was willing to share.

"We got famous," he said simply. "We got rich. Our dad showed up. Said he was entitled to our money. Made it all about him. There was a huge blow up. Damon almost got arrested. August had to straighten everything out. I don't know what he said or did, but our dad went away. We haven't seen or heard from since him."

"And that's when you started up again?"

"All that pain and anger rushed to the surface." Ian face twisted, as if the memory caused him physical pain. "Like it had just been waiting for me to give in, waiting for that trigger to go off. It only happened the once, but once was enough.

"Was it bad?"

He huffed out a dark laugh. "Yeah. I went a little nuts. I screwed up my wrists and arms. I cut too deep. Hadn't even realized at the time what I was doing. It was like I was in a trance. I snapped out of it to find myself on the bathroom floor covered in blood. It was... not good." He leaned his head back against the sofa and exhaled noisily. "I begged Damon to lie for me. We pretended it was an accident."

"How in the world could something like that be an accident?"

"Accidentally cut myself with a kitchen knife."

"You don't know how to use the kitchen."

He gave me an almost cheeky grin. "That's why it was plausible."

I let out a little laugh as the tension eased somewhat.

"The band decided to go on hiatus while I healed," Ian continued. "They didn't know I was secretly seeing a therapist. We didn't want anyone to worry. If the media got pictures of my arms, they'd think..."

"They'd think you cut yourself," I interjected, trying to dampen the hints of anger and worry in my voice. "Which is exactly what you do."

"You've seen the way paparazzi act when some starlet goes on a bender and ends up in rehab. Can you imagine the shitshow if word got out about me? Best case scenario, they follow my every move like vultures. Worst case scenario, fangirls start cutting themselves too out of some sort of sick sense of loyalty and all of a sudden Darkest Days is the reason some girl killed herself."

I could understand Ian's worry. "That doesn't mean you can't tell your friends. There's no reason why you can't tell your brother, at least."

"No." Ian's words were resolute. "Damon can't know."

"He'll want to help you."

"He already thinks he's helping."

"You said you don't talk about it."

"We don't. But... he's trying so hard. If he knew all that *Damian* shit makes it—" Ian cut himself off abruptly.

"What? Makes it what?"

"He just wants me to know I'm not alone." Ian's voice went soft. "That he's there to support me. But I get lost in it. Like I'm fading away. Like Ian doesn't exist anymore. The cutting... it reminds me of who I am. The pain belongs to *me*, no one else."

I finally understood. I understood why Ian had gotten upset all those times. Damon thought by focusing on all that *Twins* stuff, he was helping. But he wasn't. He was making it worse.

"So that's my sob story," Ian said with a rueful laugh. "Bet you didn't think you'd be getting involved with such a screw up when you proposed that fling."

"You're not a screw up," I said firmly. "Everyone has their demons to deal with, even me. Yours just happen to manifest more physically."

He gave me a curious look.

"And what about your demons?"

Chapter 28

I sat on the sofa next to Ian, motionless, not liking where this conversation was heading.

He continued speaking. "I know your mom passed away. I know your dad ignored you. I'm here for you, if there's anyone else you want to talk to me about."

There wasn't. I didn't want Ian to know how screwed up I still was emotionally. He was already dealing with so much. I didn't need to unload on him.

"I don't want to add to your worries," I finally said.

"Tell me," he insisted.

"There's nothing much to tell. I fell for a guy. I thought we really had something. He gave me all the attention I wasn't receiving at home. Then I found out he'd been lying to me the entire time."

"Is that all?"

No. It wasn't all. He told me how special I was. He said I was the only one for him. He made me think we were going to be together forever.

It had all been a lie.

"That's all," I told him.

Ian eyed me, as if he doubted my words.

"It was the usual college heartbreak," I continued, not wanting him to pry. This conversation was only dragging up bad memories and awful feelings. It only made me remember all my promises to myself not to fall for pretty words ever again.

Just like the pretty words Ian always said to me.

I shifted uncomfortably in my seat, not wanting to think about that. Ian had just shared something so personal about himself. He'd told me his deepest secret.

I didn't want to think he was lying to me about everything else.

Ian pulled me close and pressed a quick kiss on my lips. "Thank you for telling me."

"Thank you for telling me. For explaining. I don't really understand it, but I think I can accept that you have your reasons for doing what you do."

"Now that I don't need to keep my secret from you..." He twirled a piece of my hair between his fingers and brought his face close to mine. "Maybe we can start up that fling again?"

I put my hands on his chest, pushing him away.

"We still need to talk. You can't fuck me into forgetting about this."

He smirked, although there were tired lines around his eyes. "I can try."

Any protests I could have made were immediately muffled by lips crashing onto mine. Fingers tangled into my hair and fisted into my clothes. Ian's tongue played with mine, but there was nothing playful or teasing about it. The kiss was scorching, devastating. The bite of his teeth on my lower lip, a sharp hint of pain, sent a flood of liquid straight to my core.

I knew we'd have to have that conversation eventually, but Ian had seemed drained, emotionally exhausted. If this was what he needed, I'd give it to him.

I moaned into his mouth and shifted from my seat onto his lap, legs spread on either side of him. Ian's fingers skimmed the hem of my skirt up my hips. I bucked forward until the thick length of him pressed against my panties.

Ian groaned and pulled his mouth away.

"Hope, if you don't stop, I'm going to take you right here on this floor."

"I thought you needed a bed to fuck me properly."

He groaned again and plastered his mouth once more to mine. I gasped in surprised as he stood up. I clung to him, legs around his hips and arms around his neck. Two hands cupped my ass, keeping me in place. I was too occupied with his mouth to pay attention to our destination, until I went flying through the air.

I landed on a soft mattress with a whoosh of breath. Ian immediately crawled on top of me, not wanting to be parted for more than an instant.

"That fucking dress of yours." He growled and took my mouth again. "Don't you know how goddamn tempting you are?" He tore at my clothing, pulling the dress up and over my head, leaving me in my bra and panties.

"Not fair," I gasped. "You're still wearing all your clothes."

He quickly remedied that, rising up on his knees and tossing his shirt aside to join my dress. I ran my hands up his thighs until I reached his belt. Our eyes met. I unbuckled the flaps and slid it out of the loops. I fumbled to find the button and zipper. His hard cock pressed against the seam, making it difficult to draw the zipper down. His hands joined mine, helping relieve him of his pants.

He wasn't wearing underwear. My lips parted in surprise, and in hunger. His cock was hard and weeping, straining outwards. It looked even bigger than the last time I'd seen it. Maybe because this was a different angle.

"Is this the part where I kiss it better?"

"Sweetheart, you can kiss me anywhere you like."

I grasped his cock by the base and drew him forward. When he was close enough I pressed an open mouthed kiss to the flared tip. Trembling hands cupped the back of my head.

I leaned up on an elbow and took him deeper. He grunted and fisted my hair, not pulling, just grasping tight.

I flicked my tongue along the underside. Ian hissed and threw his head back.

I sucked him down until the tip hit the entrance to my throat. He cursed out loud.

I bobbed up and down steadily, taking him deep then pulling back. During one particularly erotic flick of my tongue, he let out a choked cry.

Long before I was satisfied with my ministrations, he tugged on my hair. "Stop, *stop.*"

I shook my head, his cock still buried in my throat.

"If you don't stop, I'm going to come before I get a chance to fuck you."

I let him fall out of my mouth with a loud pop. His cock was shiny and wet, solid as granite yet smooth as silk.

I wanted him inside me immediately.

He fumbled with a drawer in the nightstand and pulled out a foil packet, ripping it open with his teeth.

I hesitated for about five seconds before I put my hand on his. He paused, looking at me with a question in his eyes.

"Can I ask.... Are you—" I flushed, but continued on. "Have you been tested?"

His nostrils flared, understanding. "Fuck yeah. I got tested the minute we started sleeping together."

"Me, too. And I'm on birth control." I gave him five seconds for the words to register before reaching down and guiding him to my entrance. I was already soaked and ready for him. "I want to feel you. Skin to skin, with nothing in between us. I want to feel you coming inside me."

His eyes blazed with an inner fire. "Fuck, you're so goddamn wet." He groaned, sliding the length of his cock up and down the valley between my thighs. I spread my legs wider. Wild green eyes met mine. "You want me? You want me to fuck you?"

I nodded, moaning and squirming.

"Tell me, Hope. Tell me you want me." That voice was commanding, full of a dark, fierce passion, but I heard the plea beneath his words.

I shifted my hips until the head nudged my entrance. "I want you Ian," I gasped. "Only you."

He flexed his hips until the tip slid through my folds. "I don't think I can hold back."

"I don't want you to."

"I'm going to fuck you so hard you'll beg me to stop. You want that?"

I let out a soft groan. "God, yes..."

He slid inside with one hard thrust. I choked out a cry as his cock parted my inner walls. I clenched and throbbed around him, panting hard, trembling. My fingers dug into his shoulders, nails almost breaking skin.

He kept himself there, letting me get used to his length, his girth.

The fluttering of my muscles around his cock sent small shocks of pleasure pulsing from my core to my limbs to the very tips of my fingers and toes. He wasn't even moving and I was already overwhelmed.

When I was ready, I urged him to move with a roll of my hips. He pulled out slowly, every drag of his cock sending heat licking through me. When he pushed back in, that heat turned blazing, nearly setting me aflame.

He continued pulling out, then thrusting back in, over and over, an almost merciless pace. His cock would nearly leave me completely before the blunt head pushed back in.

He lifted my hips up until only my shoulders touched the bed. That changed the angle and sent my head spinning. His cock speared me, finding every secret spot, every hidden place, until I was mindless with desire.

A thumb found my clit, rubbing and circling and then he thrust at just the right angle and sparks of pleasure ignited my every nerve, sending me to soaring heights.

My eyes flew open as fervent passion took over. I whimpered and gasped and clawed at the skin of his back. I clenched around him, tight and warm.

That sent him over the edge. He spent himself inside me, filling me, owning me, taking over every part of me. He joined me in that delicious ecstasy as we matched moan for moan, cry for cry. We trembled and gasped and clutched each other tight, not letting go as we rode wave after wave.

Slowly, ever so slowly, as the seconds ticked by, our mutual pleasure abated and we came back down to earth. Ian moaned into my ear, a breathless plea.

"Tell me."

He was still inside me, cock still pulsing and twitching. I gripped his hips tight with my thighs, not wanting to let him go. Not yet.

"I want you, Ian. Only you."

We laid there, limbs tangled and bodies pressed together, steadily catching our breaths for what felt like hours, days, an eternity. I didn't want to leave the circle of his arms. I didn't want to wake up and face reality. I didn't want to remember the real reason why I'd come over.

I didn't want to remember the sight of Ian covered in bloody scars.

I buried my face in his chest, squirming until I could feel his heartbeat. It pumped rapidly under my ear, not slowing at all.

"Ian..." I started to speak, hesitant and not sure at all how to start a conversation like this.

His breath hitched. He tugged me closer, nearly breaking my bones with the strength of his embrace. He tucked his nose into the hollow of my throat and let out a sigh.

"We still need to talk," I continued.

"There's nothing to talk about."

Exactly what he'd said when he'd first opened the door. I didn't think it was true. If he didn't want to talk, he wouldn't have let me in. He would have continued ignoring me, shutting me out, the way he'd done when I'd broken it off.

"You said you stopped for a while. But you've started doing it again."

He let go of me and hoisted himself up. He sat on the edge of the bed, his head in his hands. "I can't let the band go on hiatus for a second time." Ian's eyes were exhausted, full of pain. He was tired of fighting. "I can't do that to them."

I crawled over and wrapped my arms around his neck, pressing my bare front to his naked back.

"At least tell your brother. Tell him you're sick and tired of the *Damian* thing. There's nothing wrong with wanting to be your own person."

"I can't. I know he feels helpless. Like there's nothing he can do to help me. He's trying. This is the only way he knows how. Besides," Ian quirked small smile. "I've only slipped up twice. I won't let it get that bad again. I promise."

"Okay." I tried to hide my unease. An inkling of an idea began to form. "I won't force you."

"Thank you." He gripped my hands for a brief moment before standing up. "I'm going to take a shower." He threw a grin my way, as if our entire conversation hadn't happened. "Care to join me?"

"I'll be there in a minute."

When he was gone, I creeped out of the bedroom to find my purse. I pulled out my phone and dialed. After a few rings he picked up.

"August? Hi, it's Hope. Can we talk?"

Chapter 29

I tapped my finger against the conference room table, nervously waiting for the members of Darkest Days to file in. I'd arrived early to set things up. I had sketches and fabric samples and market research to back me up. I wasn't sure I'd need any of it, but I wanted to be prepared. This meeting was important. Not for me, but for Ian.

I was surprised when Naomi, the band's manager, walked in with her usual impeccable suit and sleek bob. I hadn't known she'd be in the meeting, too.

"Mind if I sit in?"

"Not at all."

She pulled out a chair and sat across from me.

I hadn't spent much time with Naomi. She seemed like a competent, no-nonsense kind of person, but always with a pleasant smile on her face. Unlike Janet, who always looked like she'd eaten something sour.

"How are you finding things?" she asked.

"Good. Things are great. I'm having a lot of fun working with the band." I winced inside. Maybe she would think I was being too flippant. Work wasn't supposed to be fun.

She gave me a wide smile. "Glad to hear it. I know the guys can be trying at times. Cameron, especially."

"I can handle him."

"So I've heard. I want you to know you've been doing good work. Kristine and August have nothing but praise for you."

My heart leaped. "Thank you. That means a lot."

"I actually wanted to speak with you about that." Naomi clasped her hands together on the table and leaned forward. "I know you were originally hired for a short term internship. I don't know what your plans are beyond that, but we've been talking. What do you think about staying on and continuing to work as an Image Consultant for Etude Entertainment?"

I let out a small choking sound. "Really? That would be awesome! I'd love to. Very much."

"Wonderful. I'll speak with our team and draft something up. An official job description, employment contract with salary and health benefits."

I knew I was officially old, because the phrase *health benefits* made me go all tingly inside.

"Do I need to do anything? Talk to Janet or something?"

"No, I'll take care of it all. You continue working on the current album. Are those new sketches?" Naomi leaned forward.

I explained to her with excited motions what my new plan was. She worried for a bit, but I managed to convince her this was the best move for the band.

Although, mostly I meant it was the best move for Ian.

August wandered in a few minutes later, taking a seat beside me. He was surprised to see Naomi, glancing at her with questioning eyes. She tilted her head towards me and nodded.

August gave me a brilliant smile, the first real expression I'd seen on his face besides thoughtful or intense. "Welcome aboard."

Ian and Damon came in a few seconds later, playfully shoving at each other. I quickly glanced at Ian's wrist, but didn't see any gauze peeking out from his wrist cuff.

He caught me staring and gave a shake of his head, letting me know he hadn't done anything. I hadn't thought he would, but it was better to make sure.

"Thanks for coming, everyone," I said briskly, trying to sound professional. I was an official employee now, not just an intern.

"What's this meeting about?" Ian asked, a slightly puzzled expression on his face. I hadn't told him about it until early that morning, just before I'd left for home to get changed after another night together. I hadn't told him what I'd planned.

"Sorry for the last minute notice, but I think this is important."

"So what's up?" Damon grunted impatiently.

"I had some trouble sourcing enough material for your shattered glass concept." I was only fibbing a little. I'd had some trouble, true, but in the end I'd managed to scrounge up enough. They didn't need to know that. "So we've decided to go back to my original idea."

"We?" Damon asked, sitting up in his chair with a frown. "Who's we?"

"August and I."

Ian and Damon both flicked their eyes to August. He gave nothing away. I pressed on.

"We're going to go with torn bloody clothes for Damon to represent passionate fighting, and silk and leather for Ian to represent passionate sex."

Ian tilted his head in surprise, glancing back and forth between me and his brother.

"No." Damon shook his head. "I told you before, we want the same concept."

I looked to Ian, pleading with my eyes. Pleading with him to say something. He stared at me accusingly.

"I think this is the best direction to go in. For the band, for the concept, for everything."

I gave Ian an encouraging look. *I'm doing this for you.* Surely he had to see how important this was.

If it didn't work...

Ian closed his eyes and inhaled a deep breath. I could tell he was steeling himself.

"I like the idea."

Damon swung his head around, astonished.

"I don't want the same concept." Ian looked only at his brother as he spoke, giving him a nervous smile. "We've done the *Damian* thing for so long. This album is about trying something new. I think we should do it, Damon."

Damon's mouth popped open. Whether it was Ian calling him by his name in front of everyone, or whether it was Ian disagreeing with him, either way he was almost shocked speechless.

Damon stared Ian down, a penetrating gaze, concentrating solely on his brother. "Are you sure?"

"Positive."

They communicated without words. A bevy of expressions crossed Damon's face, not the least of which was worry. Worry and fear. He was afraid for Ian?

After a few moments, Damon nodded slowly. "Okay. Different concepts it is." He turned to me. "But you better make sure my torn clothes are sexy and not trashy. I'm not going to pull any of that Zoolander *Derelicte* shit."

Ian and Naomi snickered. August looked vaguely confused.

"No trash, I promise."

Damon narrowed his eyes at me then shrugged. "Fine. Let's run with it."

A grin spread across my face. "Perfect. I'll get working on it right away. We'll have to move fast. The album's almost done, we're already starting promotions. I need to get the material, get you both fitted again, we'll need multiple rounds of tailoring..."

"Don't kill yourself over it," Damon grumbled.

"Let me know what help you need," August told me. "I'll make sure you get it."

I had no doubt he would.

I'd spoken to August that first night I'd spent with Ian. I'd quickly run my idea by him. He hadn't been convinced at first. I had hedged, trying to explain without coming out and saying exactly why The Twins needed to have two different concepts.

I'd briefly mentioned Ian's name, saying something about how I thought it would be good for him. August had gone quiet.

After several long moments of quiet breathing over the phone, he'd agreed. We both left the real reason unspoken. I think August knew without me telling him.

It seemed not much got past August Summers.

I adjourned the meeting and gathered up my sketches, tucking them into my portfolio. Damon pulled Ian aside in the hallway.

They spoke with hushed tones, Damon with a confused expression on his face and Ian looking abashed. Slowly, his expression morphed into determination, firm and resolute.

Damon placed both hands on his brother's shoulders, bringing their foreheads together. Damon whispered a few quiet words. Ian responded with a smile. Damon pulled his brother into a hug.

I averted my eyes. When I glanced up again, Ian was gone. Damon was staring at me. Even though I was inside the office and he was out in the hallway, I took a step back, nervous, wondering what he was going to do. Wondering if he was upset with me again.

Damon tilted his head, giving me a thoughtful look, not glaring or glowering like he usually did when I was around. Instead, he lifted his chin up in acknowledgment.

Thank you, he mouthed.

My shoulders slumped in relief, no longer tense. I nodded back at him.

The corners of Damon's lips quirked up briefly as he walked away to join his twin.

Chapter 30

I walked out of the Etude building, intending to take public transit home. I hadn't expected to see Ian's expensive Spider Venom, or whatever, parked out front. I certainly hadn't expected to see Ian waiting for me. He leaned casually against the passenger side door, shades covering his eyes.

I stopped in the middle of the sidewalk, unsure how he was going to greet me. I'd gone behind his back to August. Everything had worked out in the end, though. Would Ian see it that way?

"Need a ride?" was all he said.

I bit my lip, but nodded. Ian opened the door for me. I slid in, clutching my bag nervously.

He didn't say anything as he drove. I snuck glances at him, but he didn't look my way.

After several minutes I realized we weren't going in the right direction.

"You missed the turn off," I said with a questioning tone.

"We're not going to your place."

"Oh."

Surely Ian couldn't be upset with me if he were taking me to his place.

"I want us to be able to talk in private," he added.

Oh.

My heart sank. I slumped back in my seat. Maybe he wanted to yell at me without anyone overhearing.

We made it up to his condo in silence. I fidgeted, taking off my shoes, putting my bag on an end table, checking my phone, all to avoid him. When I finally couldn't put it off anymore, I lifted my gaze to his. I found myself staring into narrowed, brilliant green eyes.

"Why?" he said simply.

"Because I was worried about you."

"I told you not to worry."

"I couldn't stand by and do nothing. If something else had happened, if you'd gotten seriously hurt, I'd never be able to forgive myself."

His mouth was twisted. He was upset with me. "Nothing else was going to happen."

"You said the whole *twins* thing made it worse. Now you don't have to worry about that. We all talked about it. Your brother agreed. No more Damian. You'll just be Ian and Damon Drake."

He stared at me silently for several long moments, before flopping onto the sofa with a heavy thump.

"I know I said The Twins thing bothered me. But I don't know if..."

I understood immediately. I went to him, tucking myself next to his side. "You don't know if you can just be Ian anymore?"

He nodded hesitantly. "We've been Damian for so long. I don't know who Ian is anymore."

I threw my arms around his neck. "I know who Ian is."

"What if just Ian isn't enough?"

"You *are* enough. You're not your brother, Ian. You're different. You're your own person. Even if no one else can see it, I can."

Ian brought his hands to my face, cupping my cheeks. "You're the only one who does."

"Soon everyone else will, too."

He leaned forward to rest his forehead against mine. "You know why I agreed to a fling?"

"Because you wanted me."

His lips curved upward. "That, too. But the real reason? I wanted time to prove myself to you."

"Prove what?"

He looked into my eyes. "I wasn't lying when I said you were special."

My heart clenched. Before, I'd brushed his words off. I'd thought they were just something he said to all the girls.

"It's like I said," he continued. "I don't want you to just be another notch on my bedpost. I thought, this girl is the first person to see me. To really see me. I thought maybe, we could have something real." Ian searched my eyes. I don't know what he saw in them, but he leaned backwards, closing his eyes and thumping his head against the wall. "You don't believe me. *Damian's* reputation makes you doubt whether I'm telling the truth or giving you a line."

I swallowed hard. I wanted to believe his words. I did.

He cracked open one eye. "You know, I don't even sleep with that many girls."

"What do you mean?" I asked, taken aback.

"All that stuff in the media about The Twins. It's almost all my brother. But since no one can tell the difference, they think we're both sleeping around."

"Ian, I've seen you flirt with anything that walks."

He gave me a small smile. "I never said I didn't use my charm to get my own way. But it's almost always Damon who's getting blowjobs backstage and taking girls back to the tour bus." He met my eyes. "I don't want you thinking I'm going to cheat on you or leave you for someone else. I don't do that kind of thing."

My heart melted in my chest a little at his reassurance.

"I have something to show you." Ian stood from the sofa and held out his hand. "Will you come?"

I hesitated for a moment before taking his hand.

Ian brought me to a room that housed a small recording studio.

"I was sort of lying in that interview." He sat me on a chair, facing him, only inches away. Our knees almost touched. He slung a guitar strap over his shoulder. An acoustic guitar, not electric. He played with the strap, adjusting it, and fiddled with the tuning before letting out a self conscious laugh.

"I don't know why I'm so nervous," he confessed.

"Did you write your own song for the album?" I guessed.

"Kind of. I wrote a song, at least. It's not going to be on the album. I wasn't going to show it to anyone. But..." he trailed off, piercing me with his gaze. "I think it might help you understand."

He put pick to strings and began to sing.

I knew how well he played, but I hadn't known Ian could sing as well. It was different from Noah. Not as gravely, not as passionate and fiery. His voice was softer. Steady yet sensual, like a slow burn.

It's all a masquerade
Can't stand the pressure

I need an escape
Need to run for shelter

I was so entranced with his voice, I wasn't paying attention to the words at first. Then their meaning drifted in.

Your searching eyes

They see what's real

What's hiding inside

I knew exactly what those words meant. My heart ached for Ian.

It was all a masquerade

Until our bodies joined together

Simply speak my name

And I'll promise you forever

My heart pounded in my chest. Was I reading him right? The meaning behind those words... was it wishful thinking?

The song ended with one final note. Ian slowly lifted his head, coming out of his trance. He met my stare, flicking his gaze from one eye to another, examining me.

I bit my lip.

I didn't want to get hurt again. I didn't want Ian to break my heart.

But as I looked at him, breathing soft, shallow breaths, seeing the longing on his face, I finally understood.

I was the one with the power to break his.

I had to let go. I had to trust. I couldn't let the past get in the way of my future.

I leaned forward and cupped Ian's cheeks, like he had mine. He parted his lips to speak. I took advantage and pressed my mouth to his in a sweet kiss. He held his breath, not moving. I pulled back and met his eyes. His face lit up, flickering between hope and wonder.

"I believe you, Ian."

Chapter 31

As soon as I said those words, the hopeful look on Ian's face eased into relief. His eyes closed. He let out a shaky breath. When he opened them again there was no hint of softness in that brilliant gold-flecked green. Relief had been replaced by a heated yearning, a deep longing that I knew was reflected in my own. He brought a hand to my cheek, stroking the line of my jaw. He pressed a gentle kiss to my lips.

My eyes fluttered closed. His hands stroked down my neck, along my shoulders, tracing my collarbone. He made his way back up, caressing my skin the whole way. He buried his fingers in my hair and tilted my head, angling it for a deeper kiss.

The breathy moan that left my mouth was almost embarrassing. My body always responded to his so quickly. I always gave in to him.

He seemed to love it though. Loved knowing how much he affected me. He crushed my body to his, leaving not a hairsbreadth between us. His lips left mine to kiss a path down my neck, to the hollow of my throat. He kissed and sucked, dipping his tongue in and out of the small indentation, mimicking the act he'd done to me so many times already.

The memory of his tongue dipping into other, more intimate places, had me trembling, anticipation and need racing through me.

He cupped my breasts, thumbs brushing back and forth against my nipples. They peaked in arousal. He bent down, bringing his mouth to my chest. He lightly nibbled on one stiff nub through the thin fabric of my dress. I shivered as a spike of heat went to the apex of my thighs.

Gentle fingers trailed down my sides to my hips, to the hem of my dress. Ian bunched it up to my waist, exposing my panties. One knee nudged between my legs. The rough scratch of his jeans against my inner thighs sent heat flooding through me. I couldn't help but grind down against him. The friction against my most sensitive spot had me reeling. An ache flared up between my legs.

He slipped underneath the elastic of my panties. I gasped as he brushed lightly against my clit. He avoided it, continuing his search until he found my already wet folds. I moaned as two fingers stroked the valley between my thighs.

"Already so wet." He sounded inordinately pleased with himself. "Can't wait to bury myself inside you."

His knee nudged me, encouraging me to part my legs further, allowing him more access. I did so, using me hands on his shoulders to keep my balance.

Those questing fingers spread me open and teased at my entrance. A single finger stroked in circles until I was bucking my hips, trying to get closer, trying to get more.

"Please," I breathed.

With a satisfied hum, Ian plunged his finger inside me. I choked out a gasp, fingers digging into the firm muscles of his shoulders. He slid in and out, rough, calloused skin rasping against my inner walls. I clenched down, pulsing around him.

He continued thrusting in and out, going faster and faster, matching the speed of my increasingly heavy breaths. I threw my head back, getting close.

He withdrew his fingers. I moaned in disappointment.

"I want you to come on my tongue."

I nearly came from those words alone.

He unzipped the back of my dress, letting it fall to the floor. A quick snap of fingers and my bra followed. He hooked his fingers in my panties and pulled them down as he knelt before me on the floor. I stepped out of them and he sent them flying. Spreading my legs wider, he leaned forward until he was inches away from me, until I could feel his warm breath on me.

He buried his face between my thighs and placed a soft kiss right above my clit. My stomach muscles clenched. He slowly dragged his tongue up between my folds. He was slow, but deliberate, licking me in just the right places, in just the right way. He continued like that, licking up and down. He knew exactly what to do to make me tremble, to make me moan. But still it wasn't enough. He wasn't paying attention to where I needed him the most.

I ground against him, rocking back and forth. He stilled me with his hands on my hips, slowing my movements, making me accept his slow pace. I whined and tugged at his hair. He let out a deep chuckle, but didn't speed up. He continued his slow, leisurely exploration of my folds.

Eventually he had enough of licking. He spread my folds with his thumbs and delved inside me as deep as he could go, dipping his tongue in and out. My legs shook as I clung to him, barely able to keep standing. The onslaught continued, repeating the motion over and over, until I was nearly mad with pleasure.

He retreated from my entrance, licking another line up my slit. Finally, his tongue reached my clit. Using the tip of his tongue he circled it, teasing and playing, until I was a panting, squirming mess. Grasping at his soft hair, I pulled him closer.

With no warning, he sucked my clit into his mouth. I cried out and tightened my grip in his hair, urging him on. That deft tongue licked and stroked, that talented mouth sucked and caressed at length. I bucked my hips, but he wouldn't go any faster, wouldn't give in to my demands to speed up.

His hands traveled up my body. He reached my nipples. Using a thumb and forefinger he tweaked them, pinching lightly. The sensation sent pleasure straight to my core. My insides throbbed and pulsed, the ache almost enough to send me over the edge.

"Ian..." I choked out his name, unable to form words, unable to plead for more.

He understood what I needed.

He slipped two fingers into me and crooked them forward, hitting a spot inside me that made stars explode across my vision. I inhaled sharply, throat closing up, not able to make a single sound as I reached my peak. My limbs trembled with the force of it. Only the grip of his hand on my hip and my hands clinging to his shoulders kept me upright.

He continued licking and sucking, easing me through it, until it was almost painful.

"S-stop. Stop." I gasped, pulling at his hair. "It's too much."

He stood, wrapping his arms around me and holding me close.

His hard length dug into my hip. He still wore his shirt and jeans. My mouth almost watered, knowing what was hidden beneath that dark denim.

"You're overdressed," I told him.

With one quick motion he flung his shirt over his head. Small indentations on his shoulders revealed where my nails has bitten into his skin, even through his thin t-shirt.

I ran my hands up and down, enjoying the warmth of those firm muscles under my fingers. I pressed a soft kiss to the center of his chest. That familiar spicy scent, something utterly masculine, made my head swim.

I wanted more of that scent. I wanted to surround myself with it. I wanted to taste it on my tongue.

I reached for the zipper on his pants. I slowly unzipped it and I lowered myself to the ground in front of him. My eyes met his as I pulled him out. His eyes burned with an inner fire as I took him in my hand.

"You gonna wrap those sweet lips around me?"

I let out a shuddering breath as I nodded.

His fingers sifted through the strands of my hair, pushing it back from my face. I leaned forward and sucked the tip into my mouth. He groaned softly, the grip in my hair tightening. I swirled my tongue around the tip, enjoying the taste of him. I closed my eyes and let out a soft moan. The vibrations went through his cock. He let out a choked sound.

"Do that again," he demanded.

I did, moaning around his cock, wanton and adoring. He groaned, sounding almost overwhelmed. I slid him further into my mouth, moaning the entire way. I made a firm circle with my lips, letting the head pop in and out, sucking on the withdrawal and licking as he slid back in.

He tugged on my hair, pulling me closer. I bobbed my head forward, taking more of him, until he reached the back of my mouth. I almost gagged, but suppressed it. He cursed again.

"Can you take me deeper, sweetness?" His voice held a hint of dark lust. "Can you take me all the way down?"

I met his eyes, my mouth still full of his cock. I nodded once. I closed my eyes again and slid down his stiff length, my lips wet and slick, making for an easy passage. Easy, until he reached my throat. I stopped short.

"Take a deep breath, sweetheart," he encouraged, stroking my hair softly.

I inhaled slowly. His hand on the back of my head urged me on. I took him deep, deeper than I ever had. His length slide along my tongue, the smooth skin of it a wonderful texture against my tongue. I concentrated on breathing shallowly, trying not to cough. Finally my nose touched his abdomen, until his cockhead was all the way down.

"Shit," he grunted. "Can't fucking believe you took my entire cock."

His hand fisted my hair, keeping me there, keeping his cock buried inside my throat for long moments. I fought not to gag, taking shallow breaths.

He tugged me back, until the tip popped out of my mouth. I took a shuddering gasp of air. I looked up through my lashes to meet his gaze.

"You taste so good," I breathed.

His eyes blazed, turning dark. He urged me forward again. I opened my mouth, letting his cock slid along my tongue, until he hit the back of my throat again. I struggled to relax the muscles, wanting him deeper. He pulled me back up, then down again, making me take him. I let him control the pace, using my lips and tongue to lick and suck whenever I could, and letting my throat relax and take him inside whenever he reached its depths.

Finally, his cock twitched and throbbed against my tongue. I knew he was close. I forced myself to take him all the way, clamping my mouth down around him and swallowing.

"Fuck!" he cursed out loud and fisted my hair in his hand. Warm, wet liquid filled my mouth, hitting the back of my throat. I savored the taste, drinking all of him down.

When he finally began to soften I pulled back. I took him in my hand and used my tongue to clean him, getting every last drop.

The grip on my hair loosed. Gentle fingers caressed my cheeks, thumbs stroking the underside of my jaw.

"Thank you," he whispered.

I stood and threw my arms around him. "There's no need to thank me. I love tasting you."

He buried his face in my neck. "I meant, thank you for believing me."

"I'm sorry it took me so long."

"I don't blame you." He let out a rueful laugh. "The Twins have a reputation."

I shook my head. "No. It wasn't that. Or, it wasn't just that. I—" I paused, wondering how much to tell him. I pulled back and met his eyes. "I got hurt, once. It almost destroyed me."

"Tell me," Ian said softly.

I settled my head on his chest. I'd never told anyone this before. Faith knew, because she'd watched the fallout. But I'd never said the words out loud before. I'd always been too hurt. Too ashamed.

"He was the kind of guy who lavished attention on me. He took me out to fancy dinners. He would give me presents almost every week."

Ian stroked my hair. "Sounds like a Cinderella story."

"It did feel like a fairy tale at the time. He told me we were meant to be. Told me how special I was."

Ian inhaled a sharp breath, no doubt remember all the times he'd said the exact same words to me.

"He was older," I continued. "Almost old enough to be my father, really. Maybe that's why what he did hurt so much. It felt like I was being rejected all over again."

"What happened?" He asked the words tentatively.

"I found out he'd been lying the entire time. I wasn't special. I was just another plaything to him. A toy to enjoy for however long I amused him, until he decided to throw me away."

I sat up, meeting Ian's eyes.

"He had an entire family I'd never known about. A wife. Three children. The house with the picket fence." Tears stung the back of my eyes. "I was just his girl on the side. Young, impressionable, willing to fall for anything and everything he told me."

Ian's face went soft with sympathy. "Hope..."

I swallowed the lump in my throat. "I should have known. Why would someone so well off and handsome and mature spend time with some nineteen year old college student?"

"You couldn't have known."

"I felt so stupid. So used. There was never going to be a happily ever after with him." I wiped the tears that fell from my eyes with the back of my hand. "I vowed I'd never fall for someone's pretty words ever again."

"I'm so sorry, Hope." Ian gathered me up in his arms, hugging me to his chest. "They were never just words for me. I always meant them."

"I know that, now." I snuggled down into his arms, waiting for the tears to subside, waiting for my cheeks to dry.

I knew that Ian was telling the truth. I felt it in my heart. But there was still one thing nagging at me. If he felt this way about me, why had he let me walk away?

"I like your song," I told him, trying to broach the subject carefully. "And not just the meaning behind the words. You're a great singer."

"I'm okay. Noah's better."

I couldn't disagree with that so I said nothing.

"I wrote it thinking you'd never get to hear it. Never thought anyone would hear it."

"Then why did you?"

"Needed to get the words out. It felt like they were choking me. Like I couldn't breathe around them."

I wanted to hear him say it. "And what words are those?"

Dark lashes swept up and down, from my eyes, to my nose to my lips. They flicked back up again until I was confronted with that brilliant green, staring deep into me, like he was examining my very soul.

"I love you, Hope."

My heart throbbed, a sweet ache. Tears stung the back of my eyes again, happy tears this time. I blinked them away. "I love you, too."

We clung to each other, basking in the words. But there were still so many unanswered questions. I spoke in a near whisper.

"If you love me, why did you agree to break it off?"

His eyes glinted, a dark look chasing away the softness, the tenderness. "Damon warned me. Told me if you saw my scars that word would get out. That you'd be horrified. That you'd leave me and tell everybody."

My throat closed. He wasn't wrong. I was close to telling someone. Anyone.

"When you called it quits, I thought maybe it was a sign. You were getting too close." He gripped me so tight I thought my lungs would burst. I didn't protest. "Letting you walk out was the worst decision I've ever made."

Even worse than cutting yourself?

I kept my thoughts to myself.

"You're the first person to see the real me," he continued. "To prove to me that I matter, even without all the *twins* stuff. You showed me I could be more than that."

"You were always more than that. You were always just Ian to me."

He laced our fingers together and tugged me close. When we were inches away he brushed his lips across mine, a soft kiss.

"Tell me."

My heart clenched, a sweet, tender ache. "I want you, Ian."

I looked up to meet his eyes, a brilliant green.

"Only you."

Epilogue

Cameron's latest party put all others to shame. He said it was to celebrate finishing the album, but he never needed an excuse to party.

There was a better mix of men and women than last time. I supposed it was because Cameron invited his fellow artists and colleagues instead of groupies and fangirls.

If I thought that meant the party would be less crazy, I would have been sorely mistaken. Celebrities partied harder than anyone I'd ever met. Broken beer bottles and shattered cocktail glasses. Couples splayed out on sofas doing indecent things to each other.

A few people in a corner snorted something up their noses. I quickly averted my eyes. I'd known drugs were a part of the lifestyle, but that didn't mean I wanted to have intimate knowledge of it.

I opened my phone and re-read Ian's latest text message.

Can't wait to see you tonight, sweetheart. It's been too long. I miss you. I love you.

That's how he ended every message now. *I love you.*

I hugged my phone to my chest. Out of all the lines Ian had given groupies and fangirls, out of all the flirting and teasing, there was one thing he'd never given them.

His heart belonged to me.

Loud music pumped from speakers situated in the ceiling of every room, a hard, driving electronic beat. I felt it in my chest, almost louder than the music at concerts.

I glanced at my sister, wondering what she thought of the whole scene. Her face was lit up with excitement. I doubted she'd ever been to a party like this one.

When Faith found out I was going to another party, she had finally called in her favor.

"I want to come too," she'd pleaded. "It's not fair you get to party with rock stars and I'm stuck doing boring corporate events with stiffs in suits. I want to live a little. Besides, it's time I finally met that famous boyfriend of yours."

When I'd asked Cameron if my sister could come, the evil glint in his eyes made me instantly want to take it back.

"No molesting my sister."

"But it's okay if she molests me, right?"

I'd just snorted. I would have paid to see Faith cut Cameron down with her barbed words.

To my surprise, it was a different rock star who ended up on the other end of Faith's tongue lashing.

She tugged on my arm to get my attention. "Oh my god, that's him." She pointed to the opposite end of the room.

"Who?"

"The asshole I keep running into. The one who thinks girls should fall at his feet to worship him."

I followed her finger with my eyes. I was speechless for a second, before I chuckled. "Let me guess. He acted like he expected you to already know him and was surprised when you didn't give him the time of day?"

"Yeah, exactly. How'd you know?"

I pulled Faith by the hand, explaining along the way. When we reached them, I tapped on their shoulders, getting their attention. Ian and Damon turned around with identical grins. As soon as they saw us, the grins slid off their faces, replaced with disbelief.

"Ian, Damon, this is my sister Faith."

They both glanced between us, slack jawed.

"My twin sister," I added.

Faith gave Damon a sweet smile. "I would say it's a pleasure, but it's really not."

"But— How—" Damon was speechless for a moment. Then he growled, a dark expression on his face. "Is that why you nearly kicked me in the balls?"

"You clearly thought I was Hope. I thought you were a narcissistic, try-hard wannabe."

A muscle in his jaw twitched. "Narcissistic?"

"You were flabbergasted when I didn't immediately throw myself at you."

"Try-hard?"

"What do you call the whole alpha male bad boy act?"

"Sweetheart, I don't need to *try* to get women to fall for me. That happens all on its own."

She put her hands on her hips. "Well it's not happening here."

Damon's face contorted. Flabbergasted was the right word for it. I doubted any girl had shot Damon down with such force in a long time.

"What's going on?" Ian wrapped an arm around my waist. I pressed a quick kiss to his lips, trying not to melt into him.

"Faith and Damon have had a few encounters before."

"Is that why he told me you were a tease?"

"Apparently he tried to come on to Faith a few times, thinking she was me."

"And I take it your sister wasn't having of any of it?"

I laughed as our siblings continued bickering at each other. Damon's brow was furrowed in a biting expression with his arms crossed over his chest. Faith's face was scrunched up with distaste, arms flailing wildly. I'd never seen her so worked up. Faith was usually so calm and collected.

"You'd think they'd hit it off, considering how well we get along," Ian mused.

"You're nothing like your brother." I wrapped my arms around his neck. "And I'm nothing like my sister."

His eyes sparked with mischief as he swung me around, keeping a tight grip on my waist.

I let out a surprised yelp, but couldn't help giggling softly.

"So, why didn't you tell me you had a twin?"

"It never came up. Also, I guess I didn't want you thinking I only liked you because I was a twin myself. My liking you had nothing to do with your twin status."

Ian settled me close to his hip. One finger trailed along my arm, up and down, causing shivers to run through me. His other hand circled around my waist, thumb brushing the hollow of my hip.

Heat surged through me, my heartbeat speeding up. I glanced around covertly, wondering if anyone would miss us if we ducked into an empty bedroom. Or bathroom. I had to admit, watching our reflections had been hot.

"I didn't tell Damon," Ian said quietly.

I pushed away my naughty thoughts. "Didn't tell him what?"

"That the whole *Damian* thing made me start cutting again."

Ian looked over at his brother with a pained expression. Damon and Faith were still arguing with each other. The situation was turning hostile, but instead of walking away, they leaned in closer to each other.

"He was trying to help. It would hurt him too much to know."

"Ian..." I wrapped my arms around his shoulders, burying my face in his chest. "I still think you should talk to someone."

"I am. I made an appointment with my old therapist. I'm going to start seeing her again." He pressed a kiss to the top of my head. "You were right. Last time I let it go on for too long. This time, I'm going to get help before it gets that bad."

A heavy weight in my chest lifted, a weight I hadn't noticed I'd been carrying around. My heart felt a million times lighter.

"Thank you," I whispered.

Bright green eyes met mine, soft and loving. "I should be the one thanking you." He brushed a strand of hair away from my face. "You saw me for who I really am. I finally feel like Ian again."

That's when I knew for sure. Things were going to be better for Ian. Maybe not perfect, but better.

There was going to be no more *Damian*. They were still brothers, still twins, but two separate people.

From now on, they were Ian and Damon Drake, the genius guitarists of Darkest Days.

From now on, he was my Ian.

***

If you or someone you know is harming themselves, please don't keep quiet. Keeping that kind of secret doesn't help you or those you care about. Seek help. Talk with a counselor or call 1-800-273-TALK (8255).

Enjoy the first chapter of Darkest Days Book #1:
Hard Rock Tease.

My heart thumped wildly in my chest. I took deep breaths to try and calm myself. It didn't work. I was going to miss my interview with Etude Entertainment. I was going to lose the best chance I had at getting my foot of the door in the music industry.

The building had too many twists and turns. The corridors all looked the same with their eggshell white walls and marble-tiled floors. Rushing around one more corner, I pushed my way through a set of double doors with shaky, clammy hands. I didn't know which way I was going, but I hoped if I continued on I'd at least find someone to ask.

Light strains of music hit my ears the moment the doors swung open. Piano music. Some of my rising anxiety eased. Maybe there was finally someone I could for directions.

Following the music down the hall, I found an open door. A quick peek inside showed me a man sitting at a piano. Broad shouldered, black hair, and tall. Even though he was sitting down I could tell when he stood he'd reveal an impressive height. No doubt much taller than me.

I was about to knock on the open doorframe when the man began to hum.

Lithe fingers spidered across the keys, a soft, tinkling melody that complimented the humming. Every so often he would stop to make a notation on a piece of paper laid flat on the top of the piano's surface.

Even without words, the man's singing was lovely. Almost sweet and romantic, somehow. The music made my heart swell, touching something inside of me. Such a sad song, yet at the same time hopeful. There was a longing beneath the light humming.

My rapid heartbeat slowed, my frazzled nerves soothed by the music. Without meaning to, I lost myself in that melody. As a music student, I could appreciate the intricacies of each note. The song didn't sound quite finished. A rough draft, maybe. Still, I could tell the man was gifted.

Hunched over the piano, his shoulders tensed up. He pressed down hard on the keys, fingers now flying. The soft melody turned harsh and aggressive. Whatever loving sentiment the man had begun with, he'd lost it. The music became louder, unpleasant. I could hear unspoken rage in the smash of every key.

The longer the man played the more discordant the notes become, until he slammed his hands down one final time, the music resolving itself in a crash of noise. I jumped, my heart beating a pounding rhythm against my ribcage.

The man buried his hands in his hair, tugging at the strands. He hunched further over the keyboard. He cursed, a quiet, forlorn expletive. Moments later he shot up from his seat at the piano with a flurry, knocking off the papers full of music notes, sending them scattered to the floor.

I took a few steps back out into the hallway, nervous adrenaline racing through my veins.

The man stood in front of the piano, his back to me, chest heaving with every breath. His hands clenched into fists at his sides. He took a slow breath in, then out. Running his hands down his face, he let out a soft, pained sound.

This man was clearly in the middle of an emotional breakdown. I didn't want to interrupt. I took a few more steps backwards, intending to leave before he noticed me.

He bent to pick up the music sheets from the floor. I saw his face for the first time.

All the air left my lungs.

This was a man I'd recognize anywhere.

Blinking once slowly to clear my eyes, I counted to three, making sure I wasn't imagining things. When I looked again, it was still him. Dressed all in black, from his open leather jacket, to his form fitting t-shirt to his tight jeans...

My eyes nearly bugged out. Damn, those were some tight jeans. My stomach muscles clenched involuntarily, an instinctive reaction. A pulse of arousal spiked through my body, warming me from the inside.

My gaze followed his body down further to his heavy black combat boots.

My heart stuttered in my chest.

It really was him.

Noah.

Fucking.

Hart.

All my senses went on high alert.

Noah Hart, lead singer of my favorite rock band Darkest Days, a rock star god, a man I admired beyond all reason, stood mere feet away from me.

My eyes travelled over his body, taking in his long legs, broad shoulders, and messy dark hair. I gnawed on my lip as excitement ran through me. He looked even hotter in person than he did on stage or on TV.

Although I had to be honest, I was sort of disappointed he wasn't wearing leather pants and eyeliner.

Pure misery showed on his face, his expression alight with inner turmoil. I held still, not making a move, not making a sound. I didn't want to disturb him in what seemed to be a private moment.

I also didn't want to risk opening my mouth and freaking out in the presence of one of my music idols.

Noah scooped the papers up, gathering them into some semblance of order. His face was open and lined with pain. The emotion he exuded on stage was just as evident in person. I wondered if he was working on a new song, if this was part of his process.

Something lit up inside my chest at the thought of Noah Hart having trouble writing songs. The fact that it might not come easy to him, despite the wondrous lyrics he wrote and the passionate way he sang, gave me a small bit of comfort. Sometimes it seemed like the work that I struggled with came about so effortlessly to everyone else.

Maybe he and I had something in common when it came to that.

I was still lingering in the doorway, watching him, drinking him in. Dark tattoos peeked out of the collar of his shirt. Enough of his upper chest was exposed to make my thighs clench. One of my shaky hands gripped the doorknob. The other was pressed to my heaving chest, feeling every one of my shallow breaths.

I shouldn't have been so affected. It wasn't like I'd never met this man or his band before. I was a fan, after all. I'd seen them backstage dozens of times. I'd shaken their hands and spoke a few words to each, gotten their autographs and given them my thanks.

I'd even seen a few members of the band up close at a private event, once. Being a music student and having friends with connections in the industry had its perks. Of course, at the time, all I'd been able to do was stare at them, mouth gaping open and blushing. It had been mortifying.

I wasn't going to let that happen again. I had to get out before I made a fool out of myself.

But I had stood in the doorway for too long. I should have left when I had a chance. Noah turned to leave. He froze as his eyes met mine.

Immediately his expression shut down, eyes shuttering. His face went blank, no trace of the pain I'd seen before.

"What are you doing here?"

"I'm so sorry," I replied immediately, shuffling my feet back and forth awkwardly.

His voice was flat. "No one's supposed to be here."

"I-I'm lost," I stammered.

The expression on his face was chilly, except for the lingering frustration in his eyes and the downturned corners of his mouth. He set down the papers he'd picked up from the floor on the piano.

"I'll just... leave," I said weakly.

Noah eyed me up and down slowly. My cheeks flushed with embarrassment at that penetrating gaze. I couldn't help eyeing him back. Damn, but those jeans were tight. I'd heard rumors, but he couldn't really be that big, could he? I could practically see his outline through the rough fabric.

"Do I know you?" he asked coldly.

I shook my head, trying to suppress the heat flaring between my legs.

"I've seen you before." The words weren't a question. "It was at a party. That album release."

My heart sank. The last thing I wanted was for him to recognize me. I didn't want him to think I was just another one of his swooning fangirls. Even if it was true.

"I remember." His eyes narrowed. "You were so starstruck you couldn't say a word."

I fought to shake myself out of my daze. Noah was right. I *had* been struck speechless before. Almost like I was now. I didn't want to let that happen again. I could pull myself together. Definitely. I could totally do that.

"Well. You know." I gestured to him.

He tapped his fingers on the top of the piano in an impatient rhythm. "No, I don't know. What?"

"You're Noah Hart," I shrugged helplessly. Noah. Fucking. Hart. I still couldn't believe it.

"You're a fan?"

I tried to make light of it. "Who isn't a fan of Darkest Days?"

"So the answer is yes?" he asked, almost mocking.

I stayed silent.

"How lucky for you to have stumbled upon me."

I swallowed hard. I was either lucky or cursed. How could I possibly manage an interview after running into the lead singer of Darkest Days? My heart felt like it might explode out of my chest. My limbs were trembling. My insides were throbbing.

I had to get a hold of myself.

"I didn't mean to intrude. I'm here for an interview."

"This area is off limits to non-employees."

"I'm sorry. I think I got off on the wrong floor."

I hovered in the doorway, unable to make myself walk away.

"You want an autograph or something?" His voice full of snark. "I can't imagine why else you'd still be standing here."

"Sorry, I'll just..." I trailed off, breath hitching as Noah strode over.

He moved like a wild animal, purposeful, with a barely restrained edge. As he approached, he scanned me up and down, his dark eyes intense. I felt my nipples tighten and peak underneath my blouse.

His eyes lingered on my chest. I had no doubt he could see the effect he was having on me. I fought back a flush.

"Or maybe you want more than an autograph?"

I folded my arms over my stiff nipples to hide them. "I don't know what you mean."

"Fangirls throw themselves at me all the time. You think I don't recognize that look you're giving me?"

"I'm not throwing myself at you. I'm just standing here."

"Your nipples are hard as a rock."

A sense of shame swirled and combined with outrage inside my chest. "It's cold in here."

"It's almost summer."

"The air conditioning is on."

"Is that why your face is red?"

I put my hands to my cheeks. "It is not."

Noah smirked. "I bet your pussy's soaked, too."

My mouth popped open, appalled and turned on at the same time. Hearing those dirty words out of this man's mouth made my inner walls pulse.

"Famous rock star or not, you don't get to makes comments on my pussy."

"Am I wrong?" He took another step forward, crowding me until my back was nearly to the wall. My breathing sped up. I couldn't even tell if I was angry or turned on. He smirked. "Have I turned you speechless again?"

I inhaled a sharp breath, but nothing came out.

He narrowed his glinting eyes at me and backed away. I let out a wavering whimper, my vocal chords beginning to work again.

Noah gave me a darkly amused look as he walked through the open door. "Good luck with your interview, fangirl."

The moment he left I clung to the doorframe, my knees going weak. Shivers ran down my spine, half in arousal and half in anxiety. I only had room for one thought in my head.

Who exactly was this Noah Hart I'd met, and what the hell happened to my soulful, romantic poet?

About The Author

Athena Wright, author of New Adult and Rock Star Romance, is a complete and utter fangirl at heart. She loves to write characters who are not always what they seem.

You can find more of her work at:
www.athenawright.com

Made in the USA
Lexington, KY
01 June 2017